Blind Date with a #FORMERPLAYER

Other Books By

Nikki A Lamers

<u>Unforgettable</u>

(Interconnected Stand Alone Series)
Unforgettable Summer
Unforgettable Nights
Unforgettable Dreams
Unforgettable Memories
Unforgettable One
Unforgettable Mistakes
An Unforgettable December

<u>Mending Shattered Hearts</u>

(Interconnected Stand Alone Series)
Breaking Cycles
The War is Over
Breaking Barriers

<u>Home</u>

Dreams Lost and Found
Finding Home

<u>Piper Falls: Station 28</u>

(Interconnected Stand Alone Series)
Leave of My Duty

<u>Waves Crashing</u>

The Lost Princess

Blind Date with a #FORMERPLAYER

A Love Canyon:

Blind Date with a #BOOKBOYFRIEND Novel

Nikki A Lamers

FREY DREAMS PUBLICATIONS

For more information, address: freydreamspublications@gmail.com

First edition, November 2025

Editor, Dina Huessini

Cover Model, Luke Brennan

Cover Photographer, Judith M Riley of Judith M Riley Photography

Cover Design, Dragonfly Design

ISBN: 978-1-951185-33-6 (paperback)

ISBN: 978-1-951185-32-9 (ebook)

www.nikkialamersauthor.com

Prologue

Aunt Miranda

Laughter rings through the open space in the back of the small romance bookstore, decorated with colorful leaves, pumpkins, ghosts and witches. The scent of apples and cinnamon fills the air like it's being piped into the room. Every store in Love Canyon goes all out with decorating each season, likely because it helps to decipher the time of year with the practically unchanging whether of the California Valley. Temperature around here tends to remain in the low seventies year round, which has me question the sanity of having the fireplace on low for ambiance.

Making my way back from the small bar in the corner, I smooth down my tan capris and cranberry red blouse with my free hand. Sitting down in a plush velvet red chair, I sip my sweet red wine and smile as I look around. The other women in attendance range in age from barely out of high school to a grandmother with two dozen grandchildren. I love looking around at all the different kinds of people it brings together. The clothing and hair styles are just as eclectic as the amazing women. We always have a good time.

The conversation drifts away from this week's read to real life book boyfriends, a topic that has remained centerstage at nearly every book club since a few of the original members took it upon themselves to play matchmaker. It's something I don't want to miss.

"What other book boyfriends do we have around here in Love Canyon?" Aggie, a sixty-seven-year-old grandmother claims, her eyes bright. "It's time to set someone else up on a blind date."

"You're right. Who knew we'd be so good at this?" Gwen, a mom of four boys under ten says, bouncing in her seat with anticipation. She's not exactly right, but she's not wrong either. The setups have gone from love to hate and everything in between.

"What about Frank from the hardware store?" Ms. Batia, my old third grade teacher suggests, wiggling her eyebrows. "He's single."

I bite my tongue to keep myself from laughing. He'd be a better match for her. "He may be a widow, but he's 75 and still deeply in love with his wife," Tanith, the owner of the bookstore states.

"We all need someone," Mrs. Batia mumbles under her breath.

"I'm sure you could help him feel better," Nora, a sweet gray-haired grandmother who lives down the street from me offers. Mrs. Batia blushes at the attention.

An idea pops into my head. I hold up my glass of wine to get everyone's attention and broadcast, "I volunteer my nephew. He just moved into the apartment in our house."

"The one that's the former baseball player?" Gwen asks with wide eyes.

"That's the one." I nod, the corners of my lips tugging up as gasps echo around the room.

"What's his name, again?" Nora questions.

"Levi. Levi Brennan. He's on Steve's side of the family."

"He's moving here? He's not going to play baseball next year?" Ms. Batia questions.

"It depends on his arm," Gwen answers before I have a chance. Everyone always knows his business. "How long is he here?"

Fighting not to roll my eyes at them, I answer, "He hasn't decided yet."

"I heard he was a different kind of player," Sacha, one of the younger women mumbles under her breath, elbowing her friend, Cilia, while a small smile plays on her lips. She's definitely getting nowhere near him if I can help it.

"Because he's surrounded by all the wrong women," I defend. I'm not naïve.

Levi has been dating a lot of different women. Women who take advantage of him and his talent. Women who want to be seen with a professional athlete or sleep with him and then share it on social media. They either want fame, money, or perks of him being a player because let's face it, they do have benefits.

"I've heard they have a name for those women," Gwen ponders. "What is it called again?"

"Cleat chasers. At least that's what it's called in baseball," I retort, pursing my lips. Everyone wants a piece of him. "And the media feeds on drama, Vegas being one of the worst. He's a good man smothered by circumstances."

The press are unrelenting vultures when it comes to him making my blood boil.

"Maybe it's time we help him find the right woman," Nora suggests.

"A good woman," I emphasize, pushing my light brown hair behind my ear.

"I'll volunteer," Rachel, a blonde, twenty-something blurts out, fanning her face as if heated at the thought. She might as well wave a sign saying she's just like all the rest. I'm sure she loves the *idea* of him, but probably wouldn't bother getting to know him.

"What about Layla Romano?" Nora proposes as if no one had spoken, giving me hope. Layla is a sweet woman and smart as a whip. "With her dad, you know she wouldn't fall at his feet because of who he is."

I stifle a laugh. That alone would help tame his ego so he can discover his footing again. He deserves to find happiness, but he's gotten a little lost along the way with so many women throwing themselves at him.

Then again, women aren't the only ones. "I think that's a fantastic idea."

"Then, it's settled," Clara, one of the original book club members announces, slapping her hand on the table in front of her like a gavel.

"What if she doesn't pick an athlete or a baseball player or something that fits him for her book boyfriend?" Nora questions.

"Then, whatever book she picks, we'll just have to find a way to make it work," Gwen insists, her eyes sparkling with mischief.

Clara focuses on Nora, inquiring about her granddaughter, Chloe. "Do you think Chloe could help us out since they are best friends?"

"I'm sure Chloe would love to help," Nora answers in lieu of her granddaughter. "What do you need from her?"

"We just need her to make sure Layla doesn't miss our next book club meeting so we can follow through with our plan."

"We can handle that," she affirms, offering me a secretive smile I happily return. "All three of us will be here."

Holding my wine glass up as if to toast Nora, my mind races with scenarios of how this will play out.

I've gotta get Levi to agree to the blind date first. This will be fun.

Chapter 1

Layla

"You don't think they're all out of control?" I ask, glancing at Chloe.

"They absolutely are, but I no longer have anything to worry about. I have my real life book boyfriend," Chloe says, smirking.

"Yeah, but you don't count with this whole book boyfriend thing."

"What's that supposed to mean?" she asks, her blue eyes bright with faux challenge. "I went on a blind date."

Glancing at her, she fights to keep a straight face even before I speak. "They set you up with Scotty, not Beck. You found Beck all on your own. That doesn't bode well for me."

Her head falls back in laughter. "Scotty is great though, isn't he?"

"Of course, and so is his husband, George, but–"

Holding her hand up, she interrupts, "Doesn't matter, they're not going to attempt to set me up anymore, so I'm in the clear."

"You are in the clear," I reiterate for emphasis and suck my lower lip between my teeth, and nervously releasing it. "They wouldn't try to set me up either. Would they? I'm not even on their radar," I claim, hoping saying the words will make it true.

She laughs. "You may attempt to be invisible, but..." she pauses for emphasis, "You're number one on my grandma's list since I met Beck."

"I know, and that's part of the reason I've been on edge at the last few book clubs. It's like my time is almost up."

"It doesn't help that you weren't at the last book club, so absolutely anything could've happened and we don't have a clue."

"Gee, thanks," I grumble, deadpan. "I was sick. The flu has been going around at school and sometimes my body can only handle so much before it caves. Besides, they probably didn't even notice I was missing."

She chuckles. "Keep telling yourself that."

A groan leaves my lips, my shoulders sagging. "Maybe we should skip."

"Now, you want to miss?"

"You've got me worried. Do you know something I don't?"

"No. It's just a feeling, but my grandmother asked if we were coming tonight and she never asks."

My stomach knots, clasping my paperback of *Fight My Fire* in front of me like a shield, I slow my steps. "Yeah, we should go home. We can grab our own wine and talk about Luke coming to put out my fire."

Chloe bursts out laughing and slings her arm around my neck, dragging me towards the front doors of the small indie romance bookstore. "We're already here."

"What about ax throwing?" I point next door.

She shakes her head, her long, dark hair flying around her while I let her tug me inside. "Remember, you love book club."

"Of course I do. Where else can you go and share something in common with someone who's barely out of high school, a mom with a full house and a grandmother in her eighties? My only hope is it stays that way."

"A blind date wouldn't change that," she insists, but I remain silent as we make our way towards the back of the store. The room is already full of mostly women, along with Scotty sitting on a couch near Chloe's grandmother talking animatedly. "There's more people here every time I come."

"You're right," I agree, my brown eyes skimming over the crowd, every face familiar.

Scotty spots us and grins, waving us over. "Let's go," Chloe urges, tipping her head towards him. We weave through everyone seated in plush chairs or curled up on beanbags on the floor with a glass of wine or a cup of tea already in hand.

"Hi," we greet them both as we approach.

Nora looks at me with wide eyes and claps her hands in delight. "You're here." She glances at Chloe. "I'm so happy you two made it."

My stomach plummets. "I'm going to grab some wine."

Scotty jumps up. "Oh, you two sit. I'll go to the bar and get us all some wine. I need to show off my glittery nails some more. They're perfect for the firefighter book tonight, don't you think?" He wiggles his fingers in front of us, his nails painted with orange and red glitter, giving them a look of fire.

"They look fabulous," Chloe agrees, grinning.

"I love them, but I'll go with you and help you carry the glasses," I offer.

Scotty plants his hands on his hip and flutters his eyelashes. "I'll be just fine, while you stay here and stop avoiding your impending setup." A soft gasp escapes my lips and my eyes widen causing him to chuckle. "Chloe told me what she thinks is going to happen tonight. It's one of the reasons I'm here. You need to sit back and soak up every second of it before we tie you to your seat."

Chloe laughs and I collapse next to her with a huff.

Tanith tries to get everyone's attention the moment he walks away. "We're going to go ahead and get started on tonight's book, Fight My Fire. What did we all think about Luke and Ali's story?"

"Makes me want to start a fire," Nora responds.

"Nana!" Chloe retorts as we all burst out laughing.

Breathing a sigh of relief as we dive into the book, I relax against the cushions, getting comfortable. Scotty returns, handing Chloe and I each a glass of wine before sitting on my other side. Licking my lips, I savor the taste of the sweet grape, and listen to everyone's thoughts on the book, remaining quiet.

I'm on my second glass of wine and believe I'm out of the woods for the night when Nora throws me under the bus. "I think it should be Layla's turn to pick a book off the book boyfriend shelf."

Instantly, my back goes ramrod straight. "My turn? What do you mean?" My stomach drops and I glare at Chloe, biting her lips to keep from laughing.

Waving my hand, I flippantly say, "You can skip me."

"We don't skip anyone," Kim, a young mom, claims.

"And the decision was already made at the last meeting," Clara, a friend of Nora argues.

"Too bad we weren't here," Chloe whispers, no longer able to hide her amusement.

"Layla never joins in," one of the three women sitting behind us mumbles, loud enough for us to hear. I'm not sure if it was Rachel, Sacha, or Cilia, but it doesn't matter. None of them have ever been nice to me. At least during breaks or summers, I had Chloe with me like I do now.

Why would they start now?

We turn in unison, Chloe opening her mouth to defend me when I put my hand on her arm to stop her. "Not worth it. We just need more wine. A lot more wine."

"Come on up here, Layla and pick a book off the shelf," Clara insists.

"What kind of man would be your perfect book boyfriend?" Nora questions, arching her brow.

"What about a baseball player?" Miranda Brennan suggests.

My eyes go wide and I jump up, knowing they will pick someone for me if I don't speak up now. "No!"

Mouths collectively snap shut around the room, eyes going wide, and staring at me. My face heats, but with my olive, Italian skin, thankfully it's hard to tell I'm blushing.

"Oh, dear," Tanith murmurs under her breath.

"I just mean...ugh, fine. I'll pick a book." I'll just grab one that's the complete opposite of who my father is. Scanning the titles on the designated book boyfriend shelf, skipping all the athletes, I pause on the #formerplayer. That has more than one meaning, but either way it's nothing like my father. He was the worst of both.

"We can pick one for you," Chloe volunteers.

Ignoring her, I sigh. "Right, what about the former player?"

Tanith hands me the book and smiles. "Good choice."

My glare turns on my best friend, her eyes alight with amusement as I slump back to my seat. "Traitor," I grumble under my breath, only succeeding in making both her and Scotty burst out laughing.

Taking a big gulp of wine, I tune out the rest of the conversation, not ready to come to grips with reality.

What the hell am I getting myself into?

Chapter 2

Levi

Finishing my workout, I stand in the living room of my temporary apartment and stretch. My aunt and uncle decorated this side of the house for guests, keeping it simple yet modern with gray and black furniture. It's comfortable with sleek lines and the space even has its own entrance.

Thankfully, they let me escape here, but it's been a while. Their house looks different, but the small town seemed to be the same as I remember when I drove through. Then again, my four hour drive had been closer to seven and my eyes were starting to cross by the time I arrived.

Stepping out my door, I look out over the backyard, taking in the patio with a large teak table and red cushioned chairs, a grill, and a U-shaped couch up against the house. Beyond, lounge chairs sit on this side of a tiered pool, water flowing down from one oversized square and into the next. It's not a pool I can swim laps in, but it is beautiful–like nothing I've ever seen.

The back door to the main house swings open and my Aunt Miranda steps onto the patio with a welcoming grin. "Good morning, Levi. I was just coming over to see if you were awake."

"Good morning. I've been up for a while. I just finished with my workout," I inform her and she nods in acknowledgment. "If I'm going to have a chance of getting my shoulder back for next season, I have to stay on top of my physical therapy." The rest of my arm is already feeling the impact of the injury and I can't let another piece of me fall apart. I'm ready to work my ass off to be in top form.

"I'm sure it will work out the way it's meant to."

Her words leave a sour taste in my mouth. I know she's only trying to support me. "Doesn't mean I can take it easy." I'm not giving up.

"True, but you'll be okay no matter what happens." I hope she's right. I'm not ready to let go of baseball, I'm only twenty-seven. "Breakfast is in the kitchen if you're hungry, but Uncle Steve already left for work."

I smile. "Thanks. You didn't have to do that."

She shrugs. "I was making it anyway. We need to eat too."

Nodding towards the pool, I change the subject. "When did you put the pool in? It looks great."

"Thank you. We added it last spring." She giggles. "Your cousins asked why we didn't put it in when they still lived here."

"Probably so we didn't break our necks wrestling from one pool to the next."

"Sounds exactly like something you and Lawson would do." A look crosses her face as if lost in a memory.

"How are Lawson and Della?" I ask about my cousins.

"They're both doing well, but we can catch up about them later. I have something to ask you."

"Okay," I say, drawing out the word.

"I need you to do me a favor."

"Of course. It's the least I can do for letting me stay here indefinitely." I give her a crooked grin.

Arching her eyebrow, she probes, "How long are you staying?"

Chuckling, I ignore her inquiry, not knowing the answer myself. "What do you need Aunt Miranda?"

She exhales harshly and holds my gaze with a steely determination, hinting that I may not like what she's about to say. "For you to go out on a blind date."

A laugh escapes and I arch my brow in disbelief. "You want me to do what?" There's no way I heard her right.

She scoffs. "Oh, don't act like it's such an inconvenience, Levi. I see you with different women all the time in the media."

My eyes narrow and my stomach twists. I expect that from other people, but not from my family–at least not here. "Don't believe everything you read."

Flushing, she waves her hand. "I'm sorry. That's not what I meant. It can't be a hardship for you to go out on a date with one woman while you're here."

Heaving a sigh, I run my hand through my hair and drop it to my hip. "Is this in exchange for staying here or something?"

"Of course not. You're our nephew. You are always welcome here and you know that. I'm just asking for a small favor, but I would never make you do it."

"A small favor is cleaning the pool, helping with dinner, or running to the store to pick up some things. It is *not* me going on a blind date," I reiterate, waiting for her to crack a smile, telling me she's joking, but it never comes.

She worries her bottom lip, as if debating on what to tell me before releasing it. "It's for my book club. They play matchmaker for some of the single women in Love Canyon, setting them up with a different book boyfriend."

My chin falls to my chest and I groan in annoyance. "Why me? I'm not anyone's book boyfriend."

Tilting her head and pursing her lips, she crosses her arms over her chest in disbelief. "You may be my nephew, but if you think that, you don't understand what book boyfriend means. And besides, the recent ego I've seen from you tells me you know better."

I scoff. "Thanks a lot."

"You know I love you, Levi, but all the women I've seen you with in the past couple years has burned a hole in my retinas and completely scarred them. I know I shouldn't take any of it seriously, but it's not you and it breaks my heart to see it."

My stomach knots. She's not wrong, but that doesn't mean I want my aunt to call me on it. "So, because you're disappointed in my choices with women, you and your book club can make me go on a date with some woman here?"

She shakes her head. "I won't *make* you do anything. I'm asking."

Closing my eyes, I exhale a heavy sigh. "I thought being in Love Canyon meant I got away from cleat chasers."

She laughs and my eyes open, veering to her. "I don't think you have anything to worry about with that."

"How am I supposed to trust that's true? Good women are a rare breed in my world and I'm pretty sure all of them are already married."

She gives me a sad smile. "Levi, I promise I wouldn't do that to you. She's a genuinely nice girl."

"Great. Just the word every guy wants to hear." My head falls back in frustration, knowing I'm going to relent. Hopefully this *nice* girl doesn't know who I am.

"Will you go? Please? I don't want her to sit and wait and have no one show. She doesn't deserve that."

I frown. Aunt Miranda knows she's getting to me. That's not something I want for anyone. "When?"

"Tonight. The diner. 5pm."

"Isn't that a little early and short notice?"

She shrugs. "You're not busy and it's when we eat around here."

My eyes widen. "When who eats around here? How old is this woman you want to set me up with?" She laughs without responding, prompting me to ask another question. "Isn't there anything better than the diner for a date around here?"

"There are a lot of great places, but we thought it would be easier since you've never met. Besides, does it matter where you go when you claim you don't even want to go on this date?"

"Guess not." Running my fingers through my brown hair, making it stick up on top, I drop my hand back to my hip in defeat. "Okay, fine. One date and one date only."

"Yes!" Grinning wide, she steps towards me and hesitates. Scrunching up her nose in displeasure, she takes a step back. "On second thought, I'll give you a thank you hug after you shower."

A laugh escapes my mouth and her features soften with both gratitude and relief. "Thank you, Levi. You won't regret this."

"I already do," I mumble under my breath as she walks away.

Chapter 3

Layla

Running my hands over my white sleeveless blouse with eyelet stitching, flared at the waist and onto my navy blue pencil skirt, I wonder if I should go home and change. I feel like I'm overdressed for the diner. Although, I didn't want to underdress for a date either. Coming on this date at all wasn't my choice, but I committed to it and I'm not backing out now. Besides, I don't want whoever they set me up with to see my reluctance the moment they lay eyes on me or think I'm over excited. I haven't been on a date in a long time. Then again, that doesn't mean anything. If I knew who they were setting me up with, it'd be easier. I've known everyone who lives in Love Canyon for most of my life. That's part of the reason I don't date anymore.

Taking a deep breath, I open the door and step inside. My eyes widen. I've never seen the diner so full. Familiar faces glance my way, a few older couples and several women from book club standing out. My eyes narrow on Chloe's grandmother sitting with her friends letting me know exactly what's going on.

This was a bad idea.

I spin on my heel and reach for the door. A hand on my arm stops me and I turn. "Hi, Layla. What a surprise seeing you here. Are you meeting Chloe?"

"Hi, Nora. I'm here for the blind date you and the rest of book club set me up with," I remind her, offering a polite smile. I don't believe for a second she doesn't already know exactly why I'm here.

"Was that tonight? Oh, well, let me walk you to a table. I saw one right over here," she says, giving my arm a gentle tug.

Reluctantly, I let her guide me to the only empty table, diagonal from her and her friends. "Thank you."

Waving to the other women, I sit down with my back to them, knowing seeing their eyes on me will only make me more nervous. Nora leans down and whispers, "Don't forget to put the rose on the table so he knows it's you."

Sitting up straight, I look around the room. "I didn't bring a rose. No one told me."

She gasps. "What? Oh, dear."

Shaking my head, I claim, "It's fine. I'm the only one here who's alone and the rest of the tables are full. I'm sure he'll figure it out." Or maybe he won't and I can leave, but with everyone here, being stood up is not ideal either.

"Okay. Good luck, Layla and have fun."

"Thanks."

Smiling brightly, she turns and walks away. Trying to forget about everyone here, I exhale slowly, getting my nerves under control.

The door to the diner swings open, gasps and murmurs hitting my ears before I lift my gaze, seeing the man behind all the chatter. My heart skips a beat.

His face isn't one I recognize, nor one I would ever forget. There's no way he's from around here. He's tall and lean with broad shoulders, and strong arms, his firm muscles on display underneath a black t-shirt. His thick, dark brown hair sticks up as if he continuously runs his hands through it making me want to do the same. Golden brown eyes roam the room and land on me causing my breath to catch.

Damn, he's gorgeous.

Gulping hard, I square my shoulders, tuck my hair behind my ear and force a smile as he approaches, hoping it looks natural. He saunters across the room, his stride exuding confidence, along with a crooked smile that nearly brings me to my knees and he knows it. "Hi, I'm looking for a rose, but... Are you waiting for a blind date?" His voice comes out deep and gravelly making my breath catch.

Nodding, my head wobbles like a bobble head and I force myself to stop. "Yes, hi. I'm Layla." Wiping my suddenly sweaty palms against my skirt, I stand, reaching out to shake his hand.

He grins wider, giving me goosebumps. Clasping my small hand in his large one, a shock goes right through me, causing me to jump. His smile falters and he drops his hands to his sides, assessing me. "Nice to meet you, Layla."

Clearing my throat, I pull myself together. "And you are?"

Taking a moment, his eyes narrow before he answers. "Levi."

"It's great meeting you."

"You look nice," he mumbles, suddenly diverting his gaze, glancing around the room instead of at me.

"Ah, thanks," I respond as more of a question. That word tends to rub me the wrong way, but I try not to let it bother me. He doesn't know that. I watch him look around, taking in our small red, white, and black retro diner as if he has something else on his mind besides this date. I can't blame him, since I didn't want to be set up either, but we're here. Why not enjoy it?

Swinging his attention back to me, he asks, "So, what's good here? You are from Love Canyon, right?"

"Yes, I grew up here. Honestly everything is good. It's basically all homemade, so it only depends on what you like."

"Then, I guess that makes sense why they picked the diner for our date. Variety and homemade cooking."

Huffing a laugh, I claim, "Or it's because they wanted to witness every part of it. I feel eyes on us from every direction."

His gaze widens and he scans the room again, a smile curving his lips. "You're right. I hadn't noticed."

"How can you not?" I question, squirming.

He shrugs. "Guess I'm used to it."

"I didn't think that was something anyone would get used to. There's no way I could."

Leaning back, he crosses his arms defensively over his chest, staring at me through narrowed eyes. "Then, what are you doing here with me?"

I scoff. "You really think highly of yourself, huh?"

"No, it's just the way it is."

Is he serious? The audacity!

"Just because you're good looking doesn't mean you have people fawning all over you."

"You think I'm good looking?" He gives me another crooked grin making me want to slap it from his face. Holding his hands up as if trying to calm a rabid beast, he claims, "I'm teasing and besides, that's not what I'm talking about."

"What are you talking about then?" I clasp my hands tightly together, forcing myself to stay glued to the chair. At least he's *nice* to look at. I hate that damn word. Everyone always assumes I'm the smart girl, or the nice one. Apparently, I'm destined to never be pretty or fun. Internally groaning, I try to stop obsessing about a word and pay attention to my date.

A teen waitress approaches us, her red hair pulled up into a high ponytail. "Are you ready to order?" she asks, pouring water into the glasses placed in front of each of us.

"May we have a couple more minutes?" Levi asks.

"Sure." She nods, turning and walking to another table.

"Look, I think we've gotten off on the wrong foot. Maybe we can start over?" His voice comes out low and soft, apologetic.

"Okay," I mutter halfheartedly, wondering if he means it.

"How'd you end up on a blind date with me?" he questions, leaning towards me as if he's truly curious about my response.

"Honestly, I think I was manipulated into it by my book club."

He laughs, bringing a genuine smile to my face. "I have to say, I'm very curious about this book club."

"It's definitely one of a kind. Why are you here?"

"The truth? I'm doing my aunt a favor."

I flinch. "Oh, how charitable of you," I mutter, sarcasm thick on my tongue.

"That doesn't mean I don't want to be here."

Tilting my head to the side, I stare at him and challenge, "Doesn't it?" He wouldn't be the only one.

Instead of answering, he redirects. "What do you do, Layla?"

Exhaling slowly, I attempt to relax my shoulders, trying to feel more comfortable with him. Maybe this isn't so bad. "I'm a physical therapist. Currently, I work mostly with all the high school sports teams and sometimes I fill in for the school nurse."

"That must be interesting."

"Sure, it's a good job. It's not exactly what I want to be doing, but my options are limited in such a small town. Don't get me wrong, I love what I do and yes, I enjoy working with the students. So many of them push too hard and end up getting hurt. I'm glad I can be there for them, and help them, but for me, it's not ideal."

His face falls and he clenches his square jaw, the movement making me squirm, both sexy and a little scary. "Really?"

Furrowing my brow, I try ignoring his obvious displeasure at my response and ask, "What about you?"

"What about me?" he snaps.

I lick my lips, attempting to ignore the reappearance of his attitude. "What do you do?"

He laughs humorlessly. "After that speech you're going to pretend like you don't know? I was told you were a *nice* girl."

"I'm not pretending anything and why do you keep using that word?"

"What word?"

"Nice," I emphasize, narrowing my eyes.

"You're acting like it's a bad word and if you're not pretending, why did you bring up how much you like working with the teams at the high school, but say it's not ideal? I can't get you a job."

A sound of pure disbelief falls from my lips. "Good because I never asked for one. Besides, I don't even know what you do."

"My aunt or uncle never mentioned that I play professional baseball for a living?" He quirks his brow.

Inhaling quickly in shock, I stare at him, eyes wide and mouth open while everything clicks into place. "You're Levi Brennan."

"Yeah, but you already knew that."

Gripping the edge of the table so tight my knuckles turn white, I lean closer, attempting to keep my emotions under control and my voice quiet. "No, I didn't. If I did, I would not be here."

He scoffs, giving me a look, telling me he doesn't believe me. "Right."

"I gave in to this blind date choosing a former player. They obviously made a mistake because that's not you."

"Well, I am a former player, but I hope that status is only temporary. Guess you're wrong on a technicality. "

"Too bad for you I don't give a damn who's right or wrong. You are the epitome of everything I don't want in a man."

"Keep saying it. Maybe I'll pretend to believe you."

"What the hell is wrong with you?" I shake my head, irrationally disappointed. For a second when he walked through the door, I actually had my hopes up, but that sure as hell didn't last. "I'm done. I don't need this."

"You think I do? I don't ever need someone to set me up on a date." His gaze narrows.

Tears burn my eyes, but I refuse to let them fall. Grinding my teeth, I push the chair back, letting it screech across the floor. I stand, glaring at him. In an instant, I no longer care about the people around us. Snatching the glass of water, I mutter under my breath, "Screw you, Levi," a moment before tossing the contents in his face.

Ignoring the gasps around the diner, I spin on my heel and storm out, knowing my name will be on everyone's tongue before I even make it home, but I don't care.

My phone rings as I slide into the front seat of my car, Chloe's name flashing on the screen as if trying to prove my point. Swiping to answer, I ask, "Why the hell would they set me up on a date with a man who's a player in every sense of the word?"

"I'm sorry, Layla. Want me to come over and you can tell me about it?"

"I appreciate the offer, but no, thanks." I'm positive she has plans with Beck tonight and I'm not about to ruin that for her. Just because I'm suffering doesn't mean she needs to.

"Are you sure?"

"Yes. I'm going to grab a tub of mint chocolate chip ice cream for dinner and read. At least the book boyfriend on the pages is one I can get behind."

She laughs. "Okay, but I'm still coming over tomorrow."

"Sounds good. Thanks Chloe. Tell Beck I said, hi." I disconnect the call and turn the key, veering away from the curb.

Maybe I didn't want to be set up, but after finally giving in, this was definitely not the way I thought tonight would end.

Chapter 4

Levi

After finally breaking away from the group of gray-haired women at the diner, I rush back to my aunt and uncle's house and change into something dry and comfortable, black shorts and a white graphic t-shirt. Tonight didn't go well. When I walked in and saw her fidgeting, looking prim and proper in her blouse and pencil skirt, my dick wanted to stand at attention. She was a vision, like every man's wet dream, making me wonder if she would let down her walls in the bedroom.

Discovering she was my date gave me hope of at least a good night, but I needed to feel her out first to find her true intentions. I'm not about to let someone take advantage of me while I'm here with my family, even a beautiful woman.

I can't believe she walked out on me. Sure, I was being an ass, but she obviously wanted to use me like everyone else. Why should I have to put up with that shit?

Maybe coming to Love Canyon was a mistake. I thought being here would give me a reprieve, but that's obviously not the case if I'm basing my decision on tonight.

The moment I flop down on the gray couch in the living room, I hear my aunt and uncle outside the door. "Just open it," she insists, her voice muffled.

"What if he's naked?" he argues.

"It's open," I call to halt their dispute.

The door flies open, hitting the backstop and bounces back. My aunt stalks over to me and without a word, smacks me on the back of the head. I flinch, rubbing the back of my head. "Hey! What was that for?"

"What is wrong with you, Levi? You were raised better than that," Aunt Miranda accuses, glaring at me.

"I didn't do anything." That's not exactly true, but she deserved it.

"You didn't push sweet Layla so she left before she ate and threw water on you?" she probes, planting her hands on her hips.

"Sweet Layla?" I dare, but she only stands taller, attempting to intimidate me. Heaving a sigh, I throw my hands up in frustration. "She only wanted something from me like everyone else."

Uncle Steve scoffs, his eyes widening in disbelief. "Layla Romano? If you think that's true, you clearly weren't listening to her."

"You're on her side too? What has she done to get everyone to have unwavering faith in her while my own family throws me to the wolves?"

"Layla is a nice girl," he declares, his jaw tight. I smirk, already knowing how much she hates that word, if her reaction when I use it is anything to go by.

"And you've turned into a complete fool," Aunt Miranda mutters under her breath. "To think I spoke so highly of you."

"I went on a date like you asked and this is what I get? She was trying to manipulate the situation," I insist, running my fingers through my hair once again.

"And how was she doing that? She didn't even know who she was being set up with." Aunt Miranda reminds me, her incredulity clear.

"She wanted me to get her a job. She was talking about how she loves working with athletes, but working at the high school wasn't ideal–"

My uncle laughs and drops down onto the recliner, leaning back like he's watching a show, while my aunt shakes her head in disappointment. "I'd think a little harder about that conversation. My guess is you're not sharing some important details."

"What more is there to know?" I challenge, not understanding why they're so adamant. "I've had people attempt to manipulate and influence me for their benefit for one reason or another most of my life. I'm pretty sure I know what that looks like."

"This time you couldn't be more wrong, Levi." Pausing, she sinks down onto the couch at the opposite end and looks at me with empathy, causing me to question myself, albeit briefly. "I think you've been spending too much time with the wrong kind of people. Apparently, listening to them has inflated your ego to an extreme even when it comes to your family, your common sense, and basic manners."

I flinch, but shake my head, refusing to believe it. "Aunt Miranda, come on. Why are you being so hard on me? You weren't there."

"You're right." She sits a little taller as if about to share something that will get me to change my mind. "But I don't have to be there to know that if all Layla Romano wanted was help with a job, she would ask her brother."

"Her brother?" I arch my eyebrow, a sick feeling suddenly twisting my gut while my mind races.

She nods. "Her brother. Gabe Romano."

My back goes rigid. "From the Mavericks?"

"That's him," Uncle Steve chimes in, pointing to me for emphasis, both of them watching me close.

"Shit," I mutter, replaying the entire conversation in my head. Have I completely lost faith in everyone, and always just assume the worst?

"Now he's got it." My uncle grins, satisfied.

"I didn't know," I mumble, still shocked. I deserved a lot worse than a glass of water thrown in my face.

"Because you didn't give her a chance. Layla deserves an apology," Aunt Miranda insists, her voice firm.

"From the sound of it, she deserves a helluva lot more than that," Uncle Steve proclaims, chuckling. "Good luck with that."

Groaning, I push off the couch, irritated at myself. They're right. I'm an asshole. I should've at least been more confident in what my aunt and uncle shared about her. They don't have any reason to lie to me.

Instead, I went and judged her based on words I twisted to fit my fucked up perception of the people in our world. I run my hand through my hair and drop it to my side. My own disappointment in myself is overwhelming even without the looks they're both giving me.

"I'm sorry," I apologize, glancing back and forth between the two of them.

"You are?" Aunt Miranda challenges.

"So, what are you going to do about it?" Uncle Steve questions, crossing his arms over his chest.

Without answering, I slip on my shoes, my thoughts already drifting back to Layla. After one look at her, it was obvious she was beautiful, but I refuse to be around another woman who wants something from me. Knowing she's the opposite of that makes her even more gorgeous in my eyes and she was already stunning.

Remembering her bright, wide, doe eyes looking back at me makes my heart race. The innocence shining in them when I threw accusations at her was genuine, but I still glared down at her with contempt.

What the fuck is wrong with me?

It's obvious she doesn't care who I am, and she won't put up with bullshit either. Layla's the exact kind of woman I didn't think existed anymore, but I would give anything to get to know better.

Yet, I just fucked it up. Damn, I really am an asshole.

Hopefully, she'll give me a chance to apologize and maybe make it up to her in other fun ways. I swipe my wallet and keys off the coffee table and stride for the door, a plan already forming in my head.

Glancing back, I ask, "So, are you going to tell me where I can find her so I can beg her for forgiveness?"

Their smiles and looks of satisfaction only confirm I'm the one who fucked up and I need to find a way to fix it. "Make sure you do right by her," Aunt Miranda insists.

Contrite, I nod my head in acceptance. Hopefully she's as nice as everyone claims when she sees my candid regret.

Chapter 5

Layla

Dressed in a pale yellow short and tank top pajama set decorated with small white daisies and a tiny lace bow at the middle of the scoop neckline, I smile at my reflection in the bathroom mirror. Maybe I'm the only one who sees me wearing them, but these pajamas leave me feeling sexy and confident. After tonight, I need that feeling. Plus, they're incredibly comfortable.

Sighing, I return to the couch and grab my book, reaching for a fluffy white blanket just as the doorbell rings. Tossing the fabric to the side, I jump up, striding for the door. "Chloe, I told you not to come," I call.

Without looking, I yank the door open and my jaw drops. A sheepish Levi stands before me, his arms full of bags. "Not Chloe."

"Definitely not," I grumble, frowning. Pushing the door, I attempt to slam it in his face.

His foot juts out, blocking it before it closes. "Please wait, Layla. I just want to apologize and then if you want me gone I'll leave."

"Fine," I mutter, too tired to argue. Spinning on my heel, I return to my spot on the couch, tucking my legs underneath me.

Crossing my arms over my chest, I narrow my eyes and bite my tongue, sitting quietly.

He steps inside and closes the door behind him, setting the bags down on the coffee table in front of me before he hands me a bouquet of pink and white carnations. "I was hoping to find you some white lilies, but I didn't have a lot of options in town, especially at this time of night. This is all the grocery store had."

"Why lilies?" I ask, curious.

Stuffing his hands in his pockets, he cocks his head to the side and watches me from underneath his long eyelashes. I refuse to be swayed by his boyish charm. "They mean forgiveness and that's something I'm begging you for."

I purse my lips, trying not to visibly react no matter how sweet I think the gesture. "You were a jerk at dinner. Why now?"

"Because I was wrong."

Slightly stunned, I sit up straight. "Did you just say you were wrong? After tonight, I didn't peg you as a man who admits his faults."

Wincing, he wipes his hand down his face and drops it to his side. "I'm sorry, Layla. It's no excuse but the world I live in can be toxic. A lot of people I've encountered will do whatever it takes to get what they want, manipulating and trampling everyone in their path, no matter the consequences."

"That's just sad."

"I'm not going to argue with you there."

"What did you even think I was trying to do?"

He grimaces peeking up at me as he admits, "Use me to help get you a job."

"That's not something I would ever do." I shake my head.

He smirks, his gaze alight with mischief when he taunts, "What about use me for sex?"

I snort, quickly covering my mouth, while my face turns a deep shade of red. Shaking it off, I ask, "What made you change your mind?"

"My aunt and uncle told me who your brother is."

I nod in understanding, but that doesn't mean I deserved to be treated like crap. I've had enough of that to last me a lifetime and I'm not about to put up with it ever again. My shoulders slump. "You know, even without my brother, I was being completely genuine. You shouldn't judge people so quickly."

"You're right. All I can do is say I'm sorry and try to make it up to you."

Staring at him, I see nothing but sincerity and regret shining in his eyes. Exhaling slowly, my body starts to relax, letting it go. "Okay, fine. I forgive you."

Levi grins brightly, the look making my breath hitch. "Thank you, Layla. I brought dinner since we never got a chance to eat." He reaches for the bags of food and begins unloading everything onto the coffee table before I say another word. "I went back to the diner. Hopefully I got it right."

My lips twitch up in amusement. "I said I forgive you, but I didn't say you could stay or that I wanted to finish our date."

His face falls and he rubs the back of his neck, tilting his head and giving me a sheepish look. "Oh, ah..."

Giggling, I let him off the hook. "I'm kidding, Levi. Sit. I'm hungry." I gesture towards the other end of the couch.

He breathes a sigh of relief and hands me my dinner before sitting down with a container of food. "I deserved that."

"This is probably better than being at the diner anyway with the whole town watching us like we were their own personal reality TV show."

"The table behind you never took their eyes off of us."

I laugh. "They're all part of the book club that set us up."

"Does that mean they had to stare at us?"

"I'm pretty sure they scheduled the date early so they could all be there to watch and attempt to eavesdrop on our conversation."

He chuckles. "So, then you don't try to get the early bird special with the seniors every time you go out to dinner?"

A snort escapes and I cover my mouth in embarrassment once again. "Sorry," I mutter, taking a bite of food.

"It's cute."

Glancing at his lopsided grin, I fight not to roll my eyes. His gaze skims over me from head to toe, giving me goosebumps. He gulps hard and clenches his jaw, lifting his liquid gold eyes to mine.

My nipples harden, suddenly reminding me of the thin fabric barely covering my flesh. Setting the food down, I scramble to yank the blanket over me before setting my container back in my lap and taking a bite.

"Cold?"

I nod and change the subject. "So, Levi, what do you do when you're not playing baseball?"

He shrugs. "During the offseason, I usually help out at camps or do motivational talks. The camps are fun, but that's not an option right now with my arm and the talks are more of an obligation."

"I get that, but can't you do the camps without playing?"

"Sure, but honestly, it's not easy to hold myself back from jumping in with the kids. Besides, they want to play baseball with us not just have us tell them what to do."

"I'm sure it's all a dream come true."

His gaze drops to his food and he takes a bite, suddenly lost in his head. "Maybe."

Hoping to bring him back to the present, I change the subject. "Do you like music?"

"Yeah."

"Movies? TV shows?"

"Of course."

"You're really not making this easy. It helps if you add a little bit of context to your answers. Are you sure you're the guy who's splashed all over the media as the player? You don't have much game."

His head falls back in laughter, the deep sound sending a chill right through me. He glances at me, his eyes sparkling. "Guess I'm used to remaining closed off. I've never had to try." I scoff and he continues, "I told you those women go after me without me doing a damn thing. Every single one of them usually only want something from me."

"Well, now you know, I'm not that kind of woman, so if you want your apology to stick, at least pretend like you're not a superficial jackass."

"Ouch."

I shrug, nonapologetic. "Look, you don't have to be here. We went on a date and it didn't work. It's fine. It happens all the time. You can tell your aunt and uncle I forgave you, but we don't have to pretend to be interested."

"Believe it or not, I'm not pretending. I am captivated by you." I arch my eyebrows, surprise and doubt coloring my thoughts. "You're beautiful, Layla. You don't give a damn who I am and you obviously don't put up with any bullshit."

Pushing my shoulders back, I emphasize, "I don't go out with players either."

"Looks like we already broke that rule." He gives me a crooked smile. "Technically, I'm no longer a player."

"You've made that painfully obvious," I tease, not able to keep a straight face.

He laughs before he brings his gaze back to mine, his eyes sparkling. "So, since you're not in danger of falling for me, go on another date with me and let me do better."

My breath catches. Delaying my response, I take a bite of the food in front of me, not tasting it as I chew. After a moment of silence, I swallow, glancing at him, his eyes still glued to me.

Before I realize what I'm saying, words spew from my lips, "I'll think about it."

He grins wide, causing my stomach to flip-flop. "That's all I ask. Would you like some dessert?"

Chapter 6

Layla

"You look happy," I observe, looking at Chloe laying back on the lounge chair in my backyard, a small smile painting her lips.

"That's because I am. What Beck did to me last night would have any woman happy, but I'm the only one who gets that pleasure."

Groaning, I run my hand over my face. "I'm really glad things are going so well for you, Chloe. You deserve it, but I'll admit, I'm a little jealous of your sex life. It's been so long since I've had an orgasm by the hands or mouth of a man that I almost forgot what it feels like."

She quirks a brow. "But not other parts?"

"Let's be real. That is only a one-eyed fictional character when it comes to giving orgasms. The concept of a cock induced toe-curling O was probably created by men who don't know how to use it."

"Oh honey, Beck and his–"

"Don't," I warn, holding up my hand.

She laughs and continues, "Well his is anything but fictional and he knows exactly how to use it. He's all man in bed. And out of it."

I scoff. "Okay, I'll believe you, but he doesn't count. He's obviously an anomaly and most importantly, he's taken by my best friend."

"Yeah, he is." She grins, her eyes sparkling.

"But what about us mere mortals?"

She shakes her head and sits up, staring at me with wide eyes as if just coming to a realization. "Wait a second. Back up. Are you saying that you've never had an orgasm during sex?"

I flinch. "No, I have, but it took some help." Pausing, I wiggle my fingers. "I'm pretty sure it's always been my nerves."

"No. You've definitely been dating the wrong men."

"Obviously."

"I should know because before I met Beck, I'm pretty sure the guys I was with were merely boys. They couldn't make me orgasm with any part of their body during sex."

"Yeah, well, you've hit the jackpot now in every way. But you know growing up here was rough for me so I didn't have a boyfriend until college. And even then, both of the guys I dated were better at foreplay than sex."

"I've learned it should never be like that unless you choose for it to be that way."

"Well, how am I supposed to find anyone when it's still the same people living in this small town? I'd rather keep to myself than date any of the guys I grew up with. The only problem, since I moved back to Love Canyon, my dating life has been nonexistent."

"There's plenty you can do to change that." I give her a look and she rolls her eyes. "I'm serious, Layla. You need a drastic modification to your life. Why don't you go out with Levi again? He looks like a man who could do the things your body needs."

My eyes narrow on her. "No."

"Why not? You said he apologized."

"He did." I laugh. "And you know why. I don't date players."

"Maybe it's time to amend that rule. You just said you told him you would think about going out with him again."

"Yeah, I said I would *think* about it."

"Don't think. Just do it."

"Chloe, even if he's not playing baseball right now, he's still all over the media with other women all the time."

"Not since he's been here."

"Which hasn't been long."

She waves her hand, brushing off my comment. "You and I both know what the media says is not always true."

"Yeah, but we also know it can hold some weight." I wince the internal scars my dad left behind aching.

"Not everyone is your father."

She knows me well. "No, but Levi is young. Too young to retire. Even though he's hurt now, he will probably get better and go back to that life. I'm not naïve. I know what that life is like."

"Not for everyone."

"No, but Levi already messed up with me. How do I trust a man like that?" I ask, my heart remembering his genuine expression when he apologized. I want to believe he means it, but should I really take that chance? And even if he does, that doesn't mean he would want more with me.

"Maybe he screwed up, but he apologized too," she reiterates, her words echoing my thoughts. "Plus, he brought you flowers, dinner, and dessert."

Ignoring her comment, I continue, "I watched my dad destroy my mom. His teammates weren't any better. So many are divorced or were never married. My brother isn't much better."

"You love your brother."

"Yeah, I do, but I don't have to go out with men like him and his teammates. I've been there and done that, trying to give him the benefit of the doubt and it didn't last for a reason."

"Dating does not mean marriage, Layla."

"Of course not, but my heart doesn't work like that. I could easily become too invested and get my heart broken. I'm not letting myself fall for an athlete."

"Fine. Then don't date him. Let him give you the orgasms you don't believe are real and he can go on his merry way."

Shaking my head, I insist, "I can't do that."

"Of course, you can, and you never know what could happen."

"He's not like Beck."

"Damn right he's not. There's only one Beck and he's all mine."

"As he should be."

Heaving a sigh, I ask, "Why are you fighting so hard for Levi? You don't even know him."

"This isn't for him. I'm fighting for you." My eyebrows draw down in confusion. "Layla, give yourself a break and allow yourself to let go. You're always concerned about everyone else. You deserve happiness."

A smile curves my lips. "Thanks, Chloe."

"Why not find some happiness under the sheets with Levi? It could be fun. Give the man a chance to at least let you see stars while he's injured. After all, since you're so hellbent on the fact that you can't fall for a player, former or otherwise, what harm could it do if you're not dating him? You get the orgasms you're after from a man who is not only sexy, but he obviously has the experience you need so you don't have to go chasing your big O. And, when he eventually leaves, both of you will be satisfied."

"That sounds like a terrible idea."

"Clearly you haven't been doing the sex thing right."

I laugh, quirking my brow. "The sex thing?"

She shrugs. "Maybe after Levi, you can relax and find a good man who delivers orgasms and treats you like royalty like my man does for me. Plus, one who doesn't have a life revolving around balls unless they're hanging between his legs. In the meantime, take advantage of his."

"You did not just say that."

She giggles and lays back down on her lounge chair. "You already walked out on the guy and he came back on his knees to apologize. Let him get on his knees for an even better reason."

"He wasn't on his knees. Besides, I'm not about to use him like other women do. I can't do that to him."

Sighing, she emphasizes, "It doesn't have to be that way if you give him a chance. I know you want to, but you're letting your rules hold you back. I'm searching for ways for you to get around them."

The thought of letting go with him feels even more terrifying and irrational than jumping into bed with him. "I don't know if I can do that either."

"Think of it this way, aren't you judging him the same way he judged you on your date by not giving him a chance?"

My heart plummets to the pit of my stomach. Groaning, my hands cover my face, disappointment in my actions nearly overwhelming me. Dropping my hands to my stomach, I huff, asking, "Why do you always have to be right?" I owe him an apology.

She laughs. "The hazards of having me as your best friend."

"Fine, I'll give him another chance."

She points to my cell. "Better text him before you change your mind." I narrow my eyes at her, but all she does is laugh harder.

Reaching for my phone, I send a text to Levi before I chicken out.

Okay.

His response is almost immediate.

Levi

Is that a yes to another date?

> Yes. What about tomorrow? We don't have school on Monday for Columbus Day.

Levi

> Perfect. I'll pick you up at noon. Wear something comfortable.

> Where are we going?

Levi

> It's a surprise.

> Is that code for you don't know yet?

Levi

> Lol.

Levi

> I can't believe I just wrote that.

A giggle falls from my lips.

> Me either. Is it too late to cancel?

Levi

> Way too late.

> Okay. I guess I'll see you tomorrow.

Levi

I'm looking forward to it.

I drop my phone in my lap, not able to fight my smile. "You look happy," she throws my words back at me. My smile immediately falls from my face and she laughs.

Great. What did I just agree to?

Chapter 7

Levi

I've never been this nervous for a date, but I really do want to make the other night up to her. I feel like such an ass. Parking my car in front of her house, I rub my hands down my blue jeans, attempting to wipe away my nerves.

This is ridiculous. I've been out with hundreds of beautiful women. But maybe that's my problem. It's been a long time since I've gone out with a woman who is not only gorgeous, but kind and I'm genuinely curious about.

Taking a deep breath, I grab the white lilies I drove two towns over to buy and climb out of the car. Straightening, I push my shoulders back, striding for her door with faux confidence and knock.

Rocking back on my heels, I wait. The door flies open, and my mouth drops as Layla steps into the doorway. Dressed in black leggings, the fabric appears like it was painted on her skin, making her legs look strong and longer than they are. A silky, evergreen, scoop-neck top curves over her full, round breasts, flaring over the waist of her leggings, barely covering the arch of her ass. Proving

I'm not an asshole might be harder than I thought. She makes something so simple look absolutely stunning making my jeans the worst thing I could be wearing.

"Hi," she smiles, her tanned skin tinging pink.

Clearing my throat, I shift to get more comfortable and force myself to meet her soft brown eyes. Her long, brown hair is pulled up in a high ponytail, a few loose curls framing her face, drawing my attention to her slender neck. "Hi, Layla. You look beautiful."

She smirks like she caught me checking her out and at the same time doesn't believe my compliment. "Thanks."

I've got my work cut out for me. "These are for you," I announce, holding out the flowers.

Her eyes soften as she looks down at the delicate petals and smiles. "You found lilies." Reaching out, she takes them from me, my hand lightly brushing hers, sparking a shock of heat to shoot up my arm. Tipping her head towards the flowers, she inhales deeply, her grin widening.

Clearing my throat, I nod. "I did. And I am really sorry for the other night. You didn't deserve that."

Lifting her gaze, she meets mine and gives me a smile. It's a look that could melt a glacier in a heartbeat, while I try to control mine. "Thank you, Levi. Wait here. I'll go put these in water."

Leaving the door open, she strides towards her kitchen. My eyes remain glued to her, watching as she walks away. The natural sway to her hips garners my attention making my mouth water. She fills a tall glass vase with water and sets it down on her counter next to a smaller vase filled with the carnations I gave her the other day. A smile curves my lips. For a moment I wondered if she might toss them after I left. Knowing she kept them gives me a little more faith in humanity, even though it likely has absolutely nothing to do with me.

She returns quickly and I ask, "You ready to go?"

"As much as I'll ever be."

She locks her door and slings a purse over her head, letting it hang across her body. Gesturing for her to go in front of me, I quickly think better of it, not wanting my dick to lead me by watching her move and quickly shuffle my feet next to her, walking side by side.

Before we reach the car, I step in front of her, opening the passenger door. Her eyes widen in surprise. "Thank you."

Smirking, I claim, "I do have manners. I'm not the animal you probably think I am."

A smile tugs at her lips. "We'll see about that." She sits down and I close the door behind her, chuckling.

Jogging around to the other side, I slip in behind the wheel and buckle my seat belt before I look over at her once again just as she drags her lip between her teeth eliciting a low groan without my consent.

"What?" she asks, arching her brow.

"Nothing," I growl, barely able to get the word out. Clenching my jaw so I don't say something stupid, I start the car and drive away from the curb, keeping my focus on the road as I head out of town.

"Where are we going?" she asks.

"It's not too far," I tell her, not ready to answer. Clearing my throat, I change the subject. "So, I wasn't very good at answering your questions before, and I want to change that." I feel her gaze on me and push forward. Opening up to anyone is not easy, but at least this time I don't believe she'll use anything she learns against me.

"How?"

In response, I start talking. "I enjoy all kinds of music, but a good rock anthem motivates me when I'm working out or preparing for a game, and I love jazz when there's no one around. It's not that I don't want to share it, but that's the kind of music that allows me to let go and relax. That's not something that's easy to do when other people are around, at least not for me."

"Levi," she begins, her tone filled with empathy.

Suddenly feeling weak, I interrupt, "I love a quiet night in watching movies or television to decompress, but I don't get a lot of time for that during the season. Honestly, it's been a long time since I've done that with anyone except someone from my family. That's something I'm usually doing alone." Pausing, I clear my throat, not daring to glance in her direction. "Sports are my go to, movies included, but ironically I'd prefer anything except baseball when I'm not working or watching game footage. I do love a good action or comedy too, depending on my mood."

"It's like you're suddenly an open book," she jokes and I give her a crooked smile. "I like it," she whispers, her voice sensual sending a shiver down my spine.

"What about you?"

"Me?"

"Yes, you. What are the things that make you Layla?" I inquire, staring through the windshield.

"Well, most of the time I like softer music, but the genre isn't necessarily important, just something calming. Lively or powerful music makes me think of girls nights, especially my best friend, Chloe." Glancing at her out of the corner of my eye, a smile touches her lips, the vision making my breath catch and I quickly force my eyes back on the road. "When it comes to movies, I want something with a good story, but I'm not big on television, I'd rather have a book in my hand."

"What do you like to read?"

"Mostly some kind of romance, but I'll read anything with a good story. Do you like to read?"

"I do, but I don't get much of a chance. I'm not sure I remember the last good book I read."

"You could always listen to an audiobook when you're traveling. You do a lot of it."

"That's a great idea. Maybe you could recommend a good book for me."

"You'll read a romance?"

"Why not?"

"Then, maybe I will," she agrees, just as a sign painted with a wagon full of pumpkins comes into view. She gasps, a bright smile lighting up her face as I drive into the dirt parking lot. "Are we going to the pumpkin farm?"

"We are. I hope that's okay?"

"It's perfect. I haven't been here since I was a kid."

My nerves loosen. I park my car along a wooden fence and reach for my sunglasses, slipping them on. "The only time I remember going to one was when I went with my cousins somewhere out here."

"Della and Lawson are your cousins, right?"

"Yeah, do you know them?"

"Not really. They seem nice, but Della is a year younger than me and Lawson is two years older."

"So, you're, what? Twenty-six?"

"Yeah," she says, drawing out the word.

"I'm a year younger than Lawson. Twenty-seven."

I jump out of my car and stride around to the other side. The door swings open as I approach and I hold my hand out, reaching down for hers. She looks up at me from underneath her long, dark lashes, hesitating before she takes it, giving me a grateful smile. Heat shoots up my arm and I try not to react.

Quickly, she drops my hand and looks away. I instantly feel the loss. The top of her head reaches just above my shoulder. She'd fit in my arms perfectly, my head resting atop hers, but I brush the thought away and focus on the moment.

I'd love the opportunity for a woman as beautiful as her to see me for me.

No, just her. I'd love Layla to see the real me.

Chapter 8

Layla

T he sweet and musky scents of flowers, apples, and pumpkins floats through the fall air, which here in the valley is anything but crisp. Oranges, reds, yellows, browns, and greens cover the grounds to add to the calming and festive ambiance. Colors of fall spread across the tables and ground off the back of an open wooden stand. Pumpkins line up in rows as if they grew from this ground, when in reality they were delivered here on a farm truck, likely similar to the one at the end of the field, overflowing with an assortment of pumpkins and gourds.

Bright mums are scattered off to the side with decorative fall wreaths, scarecrows, and hay bales. A children's play area sits in the back with a corn cob slide, a pumpkin jungle gym. a vampire merry-go-round and bat swings. "That's adorable," I say, pointing towards the back.

He grins sheepishly. "They have things for big kids too," he informs me, gesturing behind the play area. "Rumor has it they have a fantastic, haunted hayride here at night." My eyes widen and he takes a step closer. "Do you like scary things, Layla?"

"I can handle it," I retort a little too defensively making him chuckle.

"We'll have to come back one night." Reaching for my hand, he entwines our fingers, startling me. I look down at where we touch, the feeling almost foreign, but at the same time warm and soothing. Clasping his hand a little tighter, I tilt my head up and smile at him. "I thought we could pick out some pumpkins to carve later and maybe grab some snacks and wine for a picnic?"

My stomach flips. I'm surprised but delighted. "I think that's a great idea. It's been a long time since I carved pumpkins. Did you have somewhere in mind for the picnic?"

"I know a spot," he taunts, not giving me anything else.

My eyes narrow. "So do I."

He laughs and tugs me towards the meticulously displayed fields. "Come on. Let's see what we can find."

We walk side by side perusing the selection of pumpkins, while I try to ignore the tingling in my fingertips, the warmth of his palm, and the electricity shooting up my arm causing my heart to palpitate. It shouldn't feel this good, this easy, this right. "Oh, I like the big, fat ones," I say, my words echoing back in my head causing me to turn a deep shade of red, my thoughts instantly turning dirty. "Umm, I mean…"

He chuckles, but thankfully doesn't comment. "Pick any one you want and I'll carry it for you."

"No, thanks." I shake my head. "I can hold my own. Besides, carrying too much can't be good for your shoulder." My eyes veer to his arm as he rolls it in its socket, and back up to his face.

"I'll be fine, but thanks."

I find a perfectly round pumpkin and bounce on my toes in excitement. Releasing his hand, I squat down to pick it up, while Levi grabs a taller one next to mine. We set the pumpkins near the register and browse the farm fresh food and baked goods. He grabs a loaf of bread, fresh mozzarella, tomatoes, and basil, along with a bottle of sweet vinegar, while I grab a homemade apple pie believing there will be nothing better during apple season.

We return to the checkout with our arms full and smiles on our faces when the shameless whispers start and my stomach begins churning. Levi's face hardens in an instant.

"Isn't that Levi Brennan?"

"The baseball player?"

"What's he doing here?"

"More like what's he doing with her?"

"Do you think he would give me an autograph?"

"There's no way they're together. I heard he doesn't have a girlfriend."

"I bet I could get him to change his mind."

Levi spins on his heel, opening his mouth before I can even think to stop him. "I'd appreciate it if you would stop talking about my woman." I hold back my gasp at his choice of words, but I remain silent. "Hasn't anyone ever taught you basic manners? We can hear everything you're saying."

"I...I'm sorry," a blonde woman stammers. She appears to be about the same age as me wearing jeans and a white tank, but she's not someone I recognize from Love Canyon. Her gaze swings between the two of us, aghast.

The woman behind her steps forward. "Excuse me. Could I have your autograph?"

Levi scoffs, dropping cash onto the counter to pay for our items, but his eyes catch sight of a boy clinging to the woman's hand. He's maybe seven or eight and wearing a Las Vegas Lions baseball hat, his brown hair sticking out in disarray. The boy's mouth falls open and he freezes, giving his full attention to Levi.

Crouching in front of the boy, Levi asks, "Do you like baseball?"

The boy nods vehemently.

"Would you like me to sign your hat?" he asks, holding out his hand.

His eyes light up and he nearly rips it off in his excitement, handing it to Levi. "Yes, please."

Grinning, Levi pulls out a pen from what seems like nowhere. "What's your name?"

"JJ."

Levi writes the boy's name, followed by, "Dream Big" and scribbles his signature on the brim before handing it back. My heart skips a beat as JJ's face radiates his excitement. "Thank you, so much!"

Levi gives JJ a disarming smile, one causing every woman in his vicinity to melt. His good arm goes protectively around me and he guides me towards the parking lot. "Aren't we getting the stuff you just paid for?" I question, confused.

Without answering, he stops a guy wearing a shirt with the business name stitched into it, *Granny's Family Farm*. He slips him a few bills and requests, "Would you mind bringing our things out to my car?"

"No problem, Sir."

Levi grins and tilts his head down, holding me close. "If you don't want to be on camera, keep your head down and facing towards me."

My stomach flips. I didn't even notice the cell phones taking pictures until he mentioned it. The stark reminders of the similarities of Levi's life to my father's surfaces, but I do as he says. We reach his car and he opens the door for me, surprising me as his lips press against the top of my head before I slip into the passenger seat and buckle my seatbelt.

In moments, everything is packed safely in the trunk and Levi backs out of the parking lot. Giving me a sidelong glance, he slides his hand onto my knee and gently squeezes. "Sorry about that." He sneaks another look in my direction when I remain silent. "Are you okay?"

Gulping down the lump in my throat, I claim, "Yeah. I just don't understand people."

"Aren't you used to it some with your brother?"

"More so because of my dad, but yeah, Gabe too," I answer honestly, surprising myself. I never talk about my father.

"Your dad?"

"Yeah. Gino Romano. He played for the–"

Levi gasps. "Your dad was Gino Romano?" Reflexively, I flinch. "I can't believe I didn't realize it. I've seen his name connected to your brother a few times, but it's rare since your brother plays first base and your dad was a pitcher."

Heaving a sigh, I stare out the window, watching the dirt and palm trees fly by. "Gabe doesn't love being compared to him." That's an understatement, but it has more to do with not wanting anything to do with the man than it does with the sport or the athlete.

"He was incredible," he states, making me wince. My heart sinks as I tune out his chatter about my dad, but I don't stop him from talking either. I can't listen to anyone idolize my father. He doesn't deserve it. My dad is the ultimate reason this thing with Levi is a bad idea. No matter what this is.

"Layla," Levi calls as if he's been trying to get my attention.

Turning my head towards him as he puts his car in park, my eyes widen in question. "Yeah?"

Levi's eyebrows draw together in concern, his gaze searching mine. Reaching up, he brushes a loose lock of hair from my face, tucking it behind my ear. His fingers gently trail along my jaw, tilting my chin up to look at him. "I lost you there for a few minutes. Are you all right?"

"I'm fine," I answer, monotone, not able to fake it.

He stares into my eyes as if he can see into my soul. "You don't get along with your dad," he states, not questions, his voice soft, tender.

My insides prickle with awareness. Maybe he can see inside me. I shake my head, breaking our gaze. "My dad is an asshole."

Gulping hard, he nods. "I'm sorry."

I huff a humorless laugh. "You have nothing to be sorry about."

"I'm sorry I brought him up at all. I don't want to be the cause of the light disappearing from your eyes. Not ever."

A resigned sigh escapes, my gaze returning to look out the window. "Maybe you should just take me home."

"I'd rather not. I'm enjoying my time with you, Layla, and I think we can turn this date back around. We should have more privacy here for our picnic," he says sounding hopeful.

He's right. I'm not going to let my father ruin another day. So many things trigger thoughts of him, but that doesn't mean the rest of today can't be fun. Taking a deep breath, I look back at Levi, forcing a smile. "Okay. Let's go eat some apple pie."

He laughs, his relief palpable. My chest tightens and subsequently feels lighter at the deep sound. "Let's go."

Chapter 9

Levi

My gaze remains on Layla while she savors every bite of the apple pie. Her long dark lashes flutter as her eyes close, a low hum passing through her plump lips causing me to bite mine, fighting back a groan. Damn, she's beautiful and I'm pretty sure she has no fucking idea.

Uncomfortably shifting, I attempt to redirect my thoughts. "So, since you don't like baseball–"

Her body braces. "I never said I didn't like baseball, but players are another story. At least when it comes to dating them."

She's said that more than once and it raises my hackles more every time, but not against her. It makes me want to protect her from every man who ever wronged her. Apparently her father takes the number one spot on that list, but I have a feeling it might be more than that. I'm not sure she would be willing to share details for either story, at least not yet. Either way, it makes for a higher mountain for me to climb to close the distance between us when every minute I spend with her only intrigues me more, urging me to get closer.

"Okay," I start, dragging out the word, not wanting to hear her rejection. "I was just going to ask about your interest in working with the athletes at school. If you're not into sports, it seems like an odd career choice."

Her shoulders relax and she sets her fork down, wiping the corners of her mouth with a napkin and placing it on the empty plate. "Well, sometimes I think they took pity on me because I came home to help my mom when she was in an accident. I needed a job, and they hired me. Then, I just stayed."

"Is your mom okay?"

A small smile curls her lips. "Yeah, she's better now."

"Good to hear. So going back to your job, I'm confused. Did you want to stay?"

She heaves a sigh. "Before coming home, I worked at an office not far from where I went to college. It was a good job, but I gave it up to come home. Here, I have my mom, my best friend, Chloe, and my brother comes home to visit when he can."

That's not really an answer, so I try a different approach. "Do you like working with athletes?"

"Yeah, I do. I've always enjoyed watching sports. It was all we had on in our house growing up, even when my dad wasn't around. I would usually have a book with me, but I love a good game, or match, or meet, or race..."

"Even baseball?"

She giggles, the sweet sound making my hair stand on end. It's a sound I want to hear again and again. "Even baseball," she affirms. A small grin lights up my face, thinking about her watching me play, a wave of warmth rushing through me. "But I don't need anyone's help in getting a job."

I flinch. "I'm really sorry."

"No, I get it, but thank you for the apology." Pausing, she holds my gaze and proclaims, "I forgive you, Levi."

My heart squeezes. I didn't realize how much I needed to hear her say that. "Thanks," I rasp, my voice like gravel. Clearing my throat, I redirect and tease, "I can work with that. So why physical therapy?"

"It always intrigued me, especially after the first time Gabe was hurt and couldn't play. But as we got older, my brother used to get mad at me when I would analyze how someone moved and told him what they should be doing so they wouldn't get hurt, or what they could do to be a stronger and better player, especially him."

My eyes widen. "You can do that?"

She shrugs, her tanned cheeks heating. "Yeah, I guess, but most trainers and coaches can do that too. Right?"

"Yeah, to a point, but to do what you're suggesting, it takes someone who's not only smart but extremely perceptive, on top of knowing each sport."

She shakes her head, like she's diminishing what she can do. "Anyway, I use that kind of thinking when I work with the kids at school too. I love being able to help them and hopefully prevent them from getting hurt in the first place. The coaches probably don't like it, and sometimes act like I don't know what I'm talking about, but it's because they want everything to end with them. Most of them know better."

"It sounds like you're doing a lot of good."

"Thanks. I try."

"What did your brother think when you would tell him what to do?" I ask, a grin curving my lips.

A soft smile touches her mouth, her love for her brother obvious. "Gabe eventually appreciated it and sometimes he even listened."

"I'm always willing to listen," I insist, trying to catch her eyes.

She tilts her head to the side and takes a moment, staring at me before asking, "Are you sure about that? If you did, we might've actually made it to the end of our first date."

I wince as she hits her mark. "Yeah, but if we did, I'm not sure I would've been able to convince you to go on a second date with me."

"True." She licks her lips and glances behind me as if searching for a way to change the subject. "You're missing the sunset."

Taking that as an invitation, I slide around the blanket, sitting close. I hear her quick inhale while her body stiffens, just like my cock. Readjusting, I lean back on my hands, one behind her. My eyes veer to the sunset, instantly returning to her. "Beautiful."

She catches me looking at her out of the corner of her eye and attempts to hide it. Her cheeks darken. "Um, yeah, it is."

Angling towards her, a sweet, citrusy scent wafts through my nose. "I'm pretty sure you know I was talking about you," I confess, my voice low.

Ignoring my comment, she stammers, "You, um, you need to be careful. Leaning back like that will make your shoulder sore." Her eyes roam, moving from my eyes to my lips, down my arm and back.

I'm not sure if she's nervous about giving me advice, checking me out, or wondering about kissing me, but she doesn't need to be uneasy about any of it as long as she doesn't want to escape. I like her looking out for me. She's not afraid to tell me what I'm doing wrong. Sitting up taller, I let my hand fall to her thigh instead, a soft gasp falling from her lips.

"Thanks, Layla," I tell her, my voice catching unexpectedly. Looking into her eyes, the setting sun glows in her light brown orbs drawing me in.

"Levi," she whispers, breathily. "I'm just trying to help."

Nodding, I insist, "And I appreciate it." Reaching up, my fingers trace her jaw, her skin velvety smooth beneath my touch. Leisurely, my palm cups the back of her head, just beneath her ponytail, her silky hair caressing my skin. Her breathing picks up its pace, racing to catch up to the rapid pounding of my heartbeat. "Layla," I rasp, my voice rough, needy.

She whimpers, her gaze jumping from my eyes to my mouth. The tip of her pink tongue juts out and disappears much too fast. No longer able to hold back, I gently brush my lips over hers.

Pulling back, I swiftly scan her features, searching for her assent and find what I'm looking for in her rapid breaths, flushed cheeks, parted lips, liquid gold gaze, and her body angling towards me. Her head tips up to mine at the perfect angle, asking, begging for my kiss.

Goosebumps cover my flesh as I tilt my head down and seal my mouth over hers. My body instantly ignites. She gasps and take the opportunity to slip inside her hot, wet mouth. She meets me in the middle, tentative at first before her actions begin to mirror her confidence, giving in to the moment.

Her fingers weave into my hair, gently tugging, holding my head to hers as she kisses me harder. The sweet taste of apples and cinnamon fills my mouth, her tongue tangling with mine in a tantalizing, slow dance. A fiery moan leaves her lips, the titillating sound slamming into me. My already hard dick takes notice, and swiftly goes rigid.

I want more.

Sliding my right hand down her neck, and over her shoulder, the back of my knuckles graze the side of her breast. Her breath hitches and my body vibrates with need. I deepen our kiss, forgetting about where we are, Layla my only focus. Gripping her hips, I lift her towards me, setting her in my lap. She arches, grinding over my thick cock, straining behind the zipper of my jeans to break free.

Planting her palms on my chest, she sears my skin, a moment before she pushes me back. With her tanned skin flushed and her eyes full of regret, she scrambles from my lap. The look that crosses her face feels like a complete punch in the gut.

"I'm sorry," she apologizes. "I'm–"

"Don't apologize for kissing me," I interrupt, my chest irrationally tight. "There's nothing about you or that kiss that I regret and it would kill me to know I'm the only one." The words erupt before I have a chance to think.

Her eyes flicker with doubt, but she keeps her lips sealed tight, glancing away as the last of the sun's rays disappear behind the horizon.

My heart drops and I clench my jaw. If I push, this woman could eventually have the ability to shatter me, but if I hold back, I may lose the first light I've seen in someone in years and I'm not willing to let that go.

Chapter 10

Layla

What was I thinking?

Yeah, I wanted to kiss him, but the way a simple brush of his lips lit me up was nothing like I've ever felt. Chloe's right in saying he's the kind of man who could likely do things to me that would drive me wild, but with the way I responded to him, it's also dangerous for my heart. If my body is reacting like that, my heart is sure to follow. And although I said I would give him a chance, that doesn't have to mean a relationship. I can't fall for another player.

His words made me falter. He wanted to kiss me as much as I desired to kiss him but was that all it was? I'm sure he's not planning on sticking around. How could he? Preseason training will come around and by then he should be healed, ready to return to the Lions.

The atmosphere in the car feels stifling, both of us lost in thought as we drive towards my house. He turns into the driveway and parks the car. When he opens his door, I feel myself beginning to panic. My chest tightens, my palms become sweaty, my fingers tremble, my breathing picks up its pace and my eyes blur.

Calm down, Layla. You're being ridiculous.

"Um, Levi, I ah, I think I ate too much pie and I'm not feeling the best. Maybe we can carve the pumpkins another time?"

He frowns and his eyebrows furrow, giving me a look of both doubt and concern. Without a word he climbs out of the car and strides around to the other side, opening my door. Holding out his hand, he waits.

Hesitantly, I take it, pinpricks rolling up my arm at his touch. I step out of the car on shaky legs, his hand falling to the small of my back, guiding me up the walkway. "I can walk myself to the door. I'll be okay," I claim, but he ignores me.

Taking a deep breath, I unlock my door while he waits. Turning back to him, I force myself to lift my gaze, meeting his. "Thank you for today. I had a lot of fun," I say, attempting to dismiss him.

"Me too, Layla, but let's get you inside so you can rest."

I open my mouth to argue, but quickly change my mind. What's the point when the only reason I don't feel well is because apparently I'm starting to like this man and I can't let that happen? Spinning on my heel, I push my door open and step inside, Levi following close behind. "You don't have to stay. I'll be fine," I insist as I sit down on the couch and look up at him.

"I'll be right back," he says, confusing me. He walks out the front door and returns moments later with my pumpkin in his arms, setting it on the kitchen counter. Then he does the same thing with his pumpkin and the leftover food before he finally comes back to the couch and lowers himself down to my side.

"You really shouldn't be lifting so much."

"Think of it like my physical therapy."

I narrow my eyes making him chuckle. "That wouldn't be an exercise."

He smirks. "Oops. You can always punish me for it later."

My cheeks heat, and my lips twitch up in amusement while I shake my head at him attempting to ignore the dirty thoughts running through my head. "What would your therapist say?"

He chuckles and lets it go. "I'm not sure, but I don't plan on telling her."

An irrational surge of jealousy steamrolls through my insides at the thought of another woman touching him, but I swiftly push it aside. "Then, I'm telling you, you did too much bringing both of our pumpkins inside."

"I don't plan on carving mine without you," he states, watching me close while my body heats.

"Um, I'm not sure when I'm going to be up for any carving. I'm a little too shaky to play with knives."

He smirks, his look making my panties wet. Damn this man. I swear he knows exactly what he's doing. "That's okay. It doesn't have to be tonight. I can wait as long as you need me to," he insists.

My heart skitters, feeling like he's talking about more than carving pumpkins, but that's ridiculous. Desperate for a reprieve, I prompt, "Okay, well, thank you for today. I guess I'll let you know when I'm feeling better."

"Is there anything I can get you?"

"No, thank you. I'm okay. Maybe I'll feel better after I get some rest. I ate a lot more pie than I'm used to."

He sits down next to me on the couch and gives me a look, his eyes sparkling with mischief. "Are you trying to get rid of me, Layla?"

My face boils and my mouth falls open. "What? No, I just, I don't, I...ugh!" I groan in frustration.

Chuckling, he lifts my feet into his lap and takes my shoes off, one at a time, dropping them to the floor. "Since we already had plans today, let me take care of you," he requests while he tenderly digs his thumbs into the bottom of my foot. My head falls back against the cushion a moan falling from my lips. "When was the last time someone took care of you?"

It takes me a moment to process his question, but my only response is a frown. I'm not sure, but at the same time, he shouldn't be the one doing it. Nevertheless, his hands move over my feet like magic and I sink further into the couch. "I can take care of myself," I murmur, my eyes closing.

"That doesn't mean you should have to." His voice comes out gentle, gripping my heart like a vice.

Lifting my head, I hold his gaze through narrowed eyes. "Why do you care? It's not like you're going to stick around."

He grinds his teeth, acknowledging my statement. "Depends on what you define as sticking around. Yeah, I hope like hell my career isn't over and I'm able to play again. I'm way too young to retire, and still have some time left on my contract, but that doesn't mean I can't be there for the people I care about."

I gasp in surprise. Is he really saying he cares about me when we barely know each other? My stomach flip-flops. We've only been on a few dates. What does that even mean? Yes, I'm obviously attracted to him, but he has women falling all over him. I refuse to ever be just another woman in any man's bedpost, especially an athlete.

Apparently, he's really upped his game. But is that all this is to him? All I am to him–a game? Or could he really be the former player I'd been hoping for when this all began?

To stop my head from spinning, and burying myself further into the ground, I suggest, "Why don't you stay for a little while and we can watch a movie?"

Nodding, he gives me a small smile while he continues pressing his thumbs into the soles of my feet. "I'd like that."

Chapter 11

Levi

I sit in the parking lot at the high school, wondering if I made a mistake. Will she be pissed? Probably and I couldn't really blame her. Maybe she'll decide not to help. At the same time the thought enters my brain, it leaves.

Layla seems like the kind of woman that wouldn't turn someone away when they need her, even when she knows I have other options. It's obvious she has a good heart now that I've opened my damn eyes.

Last night, although she let me rub her feet, she held me at arm's length the rest of the short night. When she sent me home with a brief hug, and a light brush of her lips across my cheek, it took everything in me not to press her against the door and kiss her senseless. Something told me that a move like that would have her building impenetrable walls against me, but at the same time, I'm determined to prove her wrong. I'm not who she thinks I am. With her, I don't want to be that man anymore.

Layla is the first woman I've wanted to chase since before I got moved up to the minors and everything in my life changed in an instant. By the time I went pro, my reputation as a player shined in the media for better or worse, no matter what I did. Their claims may hold some truth, but they don't know the real me. What they say about me will not impact what I want or who I want to be anymore. I just hope Layla takes that into consideration when she hears something about me because it's bound to happen.

Taking a deep breath, I steel myself, and climb out of the car, making my way towards the football field, knowing that's where I'll find her after talking to the coach earlier. I spot her petite form almost immediately with her back to me, sticking her perfectly curved ass out to put her weight into what she's doing. A smile tugs at my lips as I watch her stretching the arm of one of the players almost twice her size. Noticing me, the players turn, one by one. I grin, waving and nodding towards their coach in appreciation.

"Heads back on the play if you don't want me adding to your suicides," their coach yells, demanding his players' attention.

The team's chatter finally turns Layla's head and her eyes widen in shock, but she quickly masks it and focuses back on the student she's assisting. Staying back, I watch her work, her gaze continuously flicking up to me. Finally, she steps away from him and he smirks, glancing in my direction before saying something to her. Her cheeks brighten and she laughs awkwardly, shaking her head before he jogs away.

Her shoulders rise and fall as if taking a deep breath before she spins on her heel, her ponytail slapping her cheek as she faces me. Her steps falter before both of us close the distance between us. "Levi. What are you doing here? I thought you had to go to therapy."

"I do." Her brow furrows in confusion and I quickly explain. "The physical therapist my team scheduled for me is a half hour drive. She's fine, but I asked her for my records and told them I had someone else in mind to take over my PT that won't have me constantly driving."

It only takes a moment before her understanding reflects back at me. Her eyes widen and she points to herself. "Me?"

"Of course, you."

"I already have a job," she emphasizes, flailing her hand dramatically towards the field.

"And helping me won't take away from that. I'll come to you and work around your schedule. Plus, you will be paid well."

"This is crazy. I don't understand. Why me?"

"Because I trust you, Layla."

I hear her quick intake of air, but I pretend not to. "Levi, I work with high school athletes, not anyone at the professional level."

"You have helped your brother."

"Not while he's been pro," she mumbles, a flicker of doubt passing through her eyes.

Hearing the vulnerability in her voice, elicits a band of pinpricks to erupt on my insides. Maintaining my gaze on her, my tone softens. "I believe you can assist me. Please, Layla. I need you."

She scoffs and looks around, as if searching for an out. Dragging her eyes to mine, she releases a resigned breath. "I don't think this is a good idea."

"This is the best idea I've had so far."

Her eyes narrow and she crosses her arms over her chest. "Don't you ever hear the word, no?"

I chuckle, rocking back on my heels. "Of course, I do. You sure as hell aren't afraid to say it to me."

She huffs a laugh. "You're unbelievable."

"Thanks."

"That wasn't a compliment."

Smirking, I shrug. "So, are you going to help me with my PT?"

I see the glimmer in her eyes the moment she decides to relent. "Ugh, fine. Do you have your files for me to review before we start?"

A broad grin spreads across my face. "I can have everything sent to you right away. Text me your email address."

Layla pulls out her phone and sends me a message immediately, glaring at her cell as if she's mad at the device she's holding in a death grip. Damn, she's adorable. Although, I don't think now is the time to tell her. I have a feeling if I shared that with her, she wouldn't be happy and I need her commitment before I step too close to the fire. Hesitating to bring up money, I ask, "We'll be fair, but don't you want to know how much it pays?" I hold my breath, anticipating her response.

"Send me the offer in your message. I have to get back to work," she claims pointing behind her.

My breath rushes out in relief knowing pay isn't a factor. Money always seems to be another contender when it comes to women who seek me out. Then again, Layla is the one hiding. "Okay. When can we start?"

"For today, do whatever exercises you were told to work on at your last appointment. After work, I'll look over your files and complete any paperwork I need to do for you or your team. We should be able to start tomorrow if everything I need is there. I'll text you where and when later tonight," she informs me, speaking fast, and glancing over her shoulder once again. "I guess I'll see you later, Levi."

Grinning from ear to ear, I nod. "Yes, you will. Thank you, Layla."

She pastes a smile on her face, her eyes still hesitant. "Goodbye, Levi." She waves and spins back towards the team.

Chuckling, I force myself to turn and walk away before she changes her mind. I'm grateful she's willing to help, I'm not about to let this blow up in my face before we even start.

At least, not if I can help it.

Chapter 12

Layla

Levi Brennan's name glares back at me. My computer screen remains lit up with his files. It's everything I need to take over his physical therapy. His injury, an x-ray, a cat scan, the doctor's and trainer's notes and the physical therapy so far. Apparently, it's not just his shoulder, he also injured his elbow, making recovery more complicated and his PT more intense.

I don't think I'm going to last with my hands on that man. This is such a bad idea. Maybe I can find someone else who can do it. I'm not about to send him back to Celia, the therapist he was using two towns over. She'd jump on advances from a man like him and I can't see him with anyone else.

Am I being over the top? Absolutely.

My cell phone rings, Chloe's name flashing across the screen. Swiping to answer, I press speaker and flop back against my couch cushions. "Hi, Chloe."

"I got your message. It sounds like you got yourself a new job," she says, giggling around her statement.

"Chloe, what am I going to do?"

"You're going to help him. Do your magic with his physical therapy and send him back to his team with his arm better than ever."

"But then I have to touch him."

"What's wrong with that? Did you forget how to do your job? That's usually how things work."

I huff, glaring although she can't see me. "Funny. It's wrong because I'm insanely attracted to Levi Brennan. He kisses like he's going to consume me and I'm going to beg for every single second of it."

Laughing, she says, "Again, there's nothing about what you're saying that tells me it's something you shouldn't be doing. Relish every moment, Layla. And if he can kiss like you're saying, just imagine what he could do between your legs."

"You're not helping." Groaning, I bury my flushed cheeks in my hands.

"I'm pretty sure that's exactly what I'm doing. Relax, Layla. You deserve to have some fun. Why not do it with Levi?"

"Chloe," I argue. "Levi is a player. He's the opposite of the kind of man I should go anywhere near."

"What happened to giving him another chance? Or just having some fun with him?"

"I'm giving him a chance to be a good friend," I claim, tasting the lie on my lips as it slips out.

Another laugh falls from her lips. "You're not kidding anyone, Layla, not even yourself. You and Levi Brennan will never be friends."

"Thanks a lot," I mutter, deadpan.

"You know what I mean. Maybe you could be more than friends? Now that is something I would believe, especially since you're his new physical therapist. Not only will you have to touch him, and rub him down, but you'll have to be spending a lot of time with him every week where it's just the two of you."

"I give up," I mutter under my breath. "I'm so screwed."

"That's what you hope."

"Sounds like you need some time with your man."

"Don't worry about me and Beck. We do just fine. This is all about you," she emphasizes. "Seriously, Layla. Stop holding yourself back. You're not helping anyone."

A knock sounds at the door. "I gotta go, Chloe, someone is at the door."

"Levi?"

"No, I'm not going to see him until tomorrow. Bye, Chloe." I disconnect and drop my phone on the coffee table.

Stalking towards the door, I yank it open, my brother standing in the doorway. His dark brown hair a little longer on top than the last time I saw him. "Gabe!" I grin, throwing my arms around his frame of five-feet and eleven-inches.

Chuckling, he hugs me back. "Hey, Squirt."

"What are you doing here? I didn't expect you to show up until after the World Series." Taking a step back, I tug him inside.

His face falls as he shuts the door behind him. "Yeah, well, since we're out now, I couldn't watch anymore. Thankfully, we were released for vacation."

"I'm glad you're here." I notice the duffle bag he dropped by the front door. "Are you staying with mom?"

He gives me a sheepish grin. Gripping the back of his neck, his brown eyes, so much like mine, reflect back at me. "I love mom, but I was kinda hoping I could stay with you."

"Of course, you can. You can have the spare room," I say, gesturing down the hall. "How long are you here?"

"I'm not sure yet. I don't have to be back until February and one of my teammates is staying at my place there."

"Anyone I know?"

"No, Jaeger came in on a trade halfway through this season. He's a good guy, but he's young and I can't deal with that shit on a day to day basis."

I grimace, thinking of Levi. "What's young?"

"Twenty-two, but he's nothing like Hurst." I wince at the mention of my ex, Cal Hurst. I've been hoping he gets traded for a long time. I want to support my brother, but it sucks feeling like I'm forced to see Cal every time I do. It's like stalking a man I want nothing to do with. "Still doesn't make it fun."

"Well, you're welcome to stay as long as you like. Did you eat dinner? Are you hungry?"

"I'm okay, thanks." He wanders over to the couch and sits down, while I lower myself on the opposite end and cross my legs, facing him. "So, what's been going on with you?"

"Um, mostly the same."

He smirks, letting me know he knows things I haven't shared. "The same? Really?"

"Basically." My face heats.

"So, you're saying getting set up with Levi Brennan on a blind date is the same old shit?"

"Ugh," I groan, scrunching my face up. "And now I'll be his physical therapist."

He arches his eyebrows in surprise. "Seriously?" I nod. "I didn't think you would work on professional players."

"Yeah. Honestly, I think I only avoided working for a professional team because of dad. Did Mom tell you about Levi?"

"Of course. That's not something she will stay quiet about."

Frowning, I confess, "It's likely one of the reasons I've been avoiding her as much as possible."

He chuckles. "How did your date go?"

I shrug. "Fine, but we won't be anything more than friends."

"You know, not everyone is dad."

"Or Hurst?"

"Definitely not," he declares, his jaw ticking.

"Sometimes that's hard to believe," I admit. "Even you are kind of a player. I love you, but you're also my brother."

"Yeah, you have to love me." He chuckles and runs his hand through his hair. "But at least I'm honest about who I am and I'm not opposed to a relationship. I just haven't found a woman I want more than sex with."

My face scrunches up in disgust. "Please, don't say that Gabe. I don't want to hear about your sex life."

"Oops." He smirks, nonapologetic.

"Besides, I don't think Levi is even looking for more and you know me, I can't do less. I'm better off not dating players."

"I'm not going to argue for the guy, I don't know him, but don't throw all baseball players in the same category as dad or Hurst."

"It's all athletes," I admit.

His eyes widen and his mouth falls open. "Seriously?"

"After dad, it's always been hard, but I think Cal shoved me over the top when it came to players. Probably because when I finally gave someone a chance, he really ruined it for me."

"That's just him Layla. He's an asshole. I'm sorry I didn't warn you away from him. I didn't know you were even dating him until it was too late."

"It's not your fault."

"Anyway, my point is that you can't rely on dad and Hurst to represent all athletes. They aren't a fair representation. A lot of the guys I've played with and against are some of the best men I know."

I nod, his affirmation confident. My thoughts stray once again to Levi. Would he want more than just a fling? I promised myself I wouldn't judge him, even though it's not easy. Do I take a chance or should I keep him at arm's length? I'm already struggling to resist him.

Chapter 13

Levi

Layla holds one hand behind my elbow and the other pushes back on my hand, stretching it. "The stronger we get everything around your elbow and shoulder, the better it will be," she explains. Her fingers slide down my arm eliciting goosebumps and causing me to release a harsh exhale. I love having her touch me, but preferably not for this.

"I get it. Unfortunately, I've had enough injuries in my lifetime that I understand the importance of listening to you." Her soft brown orbs stare into mine making my heart race. Why did I ever think that Layla seeing me at some of my worst moments was a good idea?

Tearing her gaze away from mine, she steps away and reaches into a small freezer, pulling out two blue ice packs and slipping each one into a thin sleeve before shuffling back to me. I wince as she places ice on my shoulder and elbow. "Just rest with these packs for twenty minutes and then you're done for today."

"This was your initial assessment?"

She nods. "I didn't need to do a full assessment. Most of what I did was more for me to see for myself. Your team physical therapists and the one you went to down the road left a lot of notes, plus your medical records. If I didn't do that, I wouldn't know that it was both your shoulder and your elbow."

"Yeah, I guess one injury led to another."

"That makes sense. I'm also assuming you do all your exercises at home?" She pauses and I nod. "Good, but I'm glad I could evaluate you and get you going before too much time passed."

"I promise, I've been doing everything I'm told. I'm not taking any chances. I want my arm back at its best. My career depends on it. Besides, you sure as hell didn't take it easy on me."

She arches her eyebrows and crosses her arms defensively over her chest. "If you don't want to be pushed, I'm not who you want."

"I can respect that, but you're definitely exactly who I want and who I need." Her cheeks heat, giving me my intended effect.

Flustered, she rephrases, stammering, "I um, I will get you back where you want to be. Your arm is fixable, both your shoulder and your elbow, as long as you do the work."

"I wouldn't have it any other way."

"Good."

"So, would you like to go out with me this weekend? We could go on the haunted hayride, and maybe grab something to eat?" I propose, watching her in amusement as she suddenly becomes super busy with the paperwork I'm almost positive is already complete.

Without looking at me, she mumbles a response. "I'm not sure if that's a good idea, Levi."

"Haven't we already talked about this, Layla? It's a fantastic idea."

Finally meeting my gaze, she pushes her shoulders back and insists, "We should keep this professional now that I'm your physical therapist."

Chuckling, I shake my head. "You're not using this to get between us. I'll find another physical therapist before I let that happen. My PT is not an excuse to keep me at bay."

"It's not an excuse."

I arch my eyebrows in challenge. We both know exactly what she's doing. "What about dinner tonight? You have to eat."

"My brother is in town. He got in late last night and I should really have dinner with him tonight."

Her phone pings, and I notice her brother's name flashing on the screen, bringing a smile to my face. "That sounds great to me. I'd love to get to know your brother. We obviously have a lot in common and I've only ever played against him. He's a fantastic player." I pause, and she stares at me, dumbfounded. "He's texting you now," I advise, nodding towards her cell.

She grabs her phone and huffs, frowning as she reads. "Um... He can't. Evidently, he has a date."

My grin grows. "So, that means you're available to go out to dinner with me tonight."

"Apparently," she grumbles causing me to burst out laughing only making her glare intensify.

Swallowing my amusement, I tease, "Good to know it's such a hardship to have a meal with me."

Her face falls, turning apologetic. "It's not like that, Levi."

"It's okay. I know you don't mean anything by it, but I promise, I will make it worth your while."

"You really don't give up, do you?"

"When it comes to you, I don't plan on it."

A giggle escapes, but she quickly covers it up, turning it into a cough. "Okay. I will have dinner with you tonight, but would it be okay if we do take out instead? It's been a long week."

"Yeah, I like that plan. Better yet, I'll cook you dinner."

Her eyes widen, brightening, letting me know I'm making the right decision. "That sounds wonderful. I can't say no to that."

"Good. I have to go to the grocery store and run home to take a quick shower. After that I could come pick you up?"

"I can drive over to your aunt and uncle's."

"Let me pick you up. My place is attached to their house. I'd rather show you inside than have you come in through their front door or wander through the back yard to get to me the first time."

"Okay."

"Do you have any allergies or anything you won't eat?"

"No. I don't think so."

"Good. Then, I'll be over around 6:30."

"All right." She shakes her head in disbelief, as if trying to figure out what just happened. "Keep the ice packs on your arm. You still have another ten minutes. I'll be right back."

A smile curves my lips as I watch her walk out of the room. I feel like I'm making progress. One step at a time. Hopefully, I can keep moving in this direction when it comes to Layla.

Chapter 14

Layla

Knowing I don't have enough time to dry my hair, I brush it up into a high ponytail and take a quick look in the mirror. My cheeks are flushed underneath my neutral makeup, keeping it simple. Rushing to my closet, I stand in my matching red lace bra and panty set, the sexy lingerie increasing my confidence. I need something to give it a boost when Levi is around, even if I'm the only one who sees it. He leaves me on edge and burning with desire, salivating like I'm the modern day kissing bandit ready to pounce and chase him around the bases.

I'm stronger than that. I can have dinner with a gorgeous man at his place without trying to jump him. I do it all the time. Well, that's not true, but I could and it wouldn't be a big deal. So why does Levi feel different? Brushing the question away, I search through my clothes, wanting to be cute and comfortable without looking like I'm trying.

Ugh. What the hell am I supposed to wear? Trying not to think too hard, I grab a pale pink, short-sleeve, cotton dress, with a collar and two of the three buttons open. The fabric skims my thigh as I slip it on. A knock at the door, grabs my attention while I slip on silver sandals. Glancing in the mirror one more time on the way out of my room, I stride for the door.

Yanking it open, I smile at Levi. "Hi."

His eyes flare as they swiftly roam my body before meeting my gaze. He gulps, his Adam's apple bobbing up and down. "Hi," he says, his voice cracking. Pausing, he clears his throat. "You look beautiful."

"Thank you."

"Are you ready?"

"Yup." I step outside and tug my door shut, locking it behind me.

Spinning towards the sidewalk, his hand falls to the small of my back, his light touch like an electric charge causing my hair to stand on end. When I lift my gaze, my steps falter. "Um, where's your car?"

He gives me a crooked grin making my heart stutter. "It's only two blocks. I thought we could walk."

My face heats. "Oh, sure. It's the perfect evening for it, but you should've let me walk over. I forgot you were so close."

"It's time I get to spend with you."

A giggle slips out before I can stop it making me blush. "Sorry but I couldn't help it. That sounds like another line."

He chuckles. "Is it working?"

My heart stutters but I try to ignore it. Instead of answering, I attempt to redirect the conversation. "So, what are you making for dinner? Peanut butter and jelly sandwiches?"

His eyes spark with amusement. "I do love PB and J." We both laugh. "Believe it or not, I can cook."

"Well, I guess I'll find out soon enough."

We walk through a gate on the side of the house, the soft glow of lanterns lighting the path. The calming sound of small waterfalls spilling into a pool below brings a smile to my face. "Wow, this outdoor space is incredible."

"Yeah, I think so too. They did all this after my cousins moved out." He gestures to a door on the right. "This is where I'm staying while I'm here."

He opens it and I step inside, the apartment modern, yet warm. With the lack of personal pictures on the walls, I'm surprised by how cozy it feels. Maybe it's the salty and masculine scent of Levi permeating my senses or seeing a baseball bag and shoes stacked on a bench near the front door. Or it could be the small, oval, oak table between the living room and kitchen set with navy blue cloth placemats, white napkins, candles and a small bouquet of blue and white hydrangeas bringing a smile to my face.

"This is a fantastic space."

"It is, but it's definitely designed for guests. Although, my Aunt Miranda put a picture of my cousins and me in the hallway."

"Is the table design for guests too?" I smirk.

"That might be my doing."

"Might be?"

He gives me a crooked smile making my breath catch. "Do you want something to drink while I finish up dinner?"

He walks backwards towards the kitchen, keeping his eyes on me. "What do you have?" I follow him, pausing in the doorway.

"Water, beer, red wine, white wine, rosé..." he trails off, hesitating. "If I didn't know you were coming there'd likely be a few less choices."

Giggling, I answer, "I would love a glass of chardonnay if you have it." He nods, my eyes remaining on him, watching as he reaches for two clear glasses and swiftly pops the cork. He pours a glass for each of us and hands me one, his fingers brushing mine, eliciting goosebumps.

"To getting to know each other better," he proclaims, holding my stare.

A shiver runs down my spine and I let out a shaky breath, tipping my wineglass to his. "I'll drink to that." As the light clink echoes in the room, I tear my eyes from his, attempting to calm my nerves. I take a sip, the dry, oaky flavors accented with a hint of peach dance on my tongue.

"What do you think?"

I lick my lips and his gaze follows the movement making me gasp. "It's good. I like it."

Taking a deep breath, he spins away from me and sets his glass down. "Good, good," he murmurs, turning on the stove. Lifting the lid off a large skillet, he grabs a serving spoon and stirs, the savory aroma of its contents hitting me.

Closing my eyes, I inhale deeply. "That smells so good," I croon, opening my eyes and staring at him. "What are you making?"

Satisfaction and happiness dance in his eyes. "Shrimp orzo. It's garlic sautéed shrimp with the orzo cooked in clam juice, blended with peas, sun-dried tomatoes, spinach, cream, lemon..." He pauses, glancing at me. "We weren't gone long, so it will be ready soon. I think you'll like it."

"It sounds incredible and smells even better."

His cheeks heat, surprising me. "Thanks."

"So, you like to cook?"

"Yeah, I guess it made things easier."

My eyebrows draw down in confusion. "What do you mean?"

He chuckles and waves his hand in the air as if it's no big deal, but something in his eyes tells me that's not the case. "I was a teenage boy and an athlete. I ate a lot." He laughs again, but it sounds hollow.

"You learned young."

"Yeah. What about you? Do you like to cook?"

"I do, but I can't cook anything fancy like this."

He chuckles. "This isn't fancy."

"It is to me."

"Well, as long as you like it, I'll be happy." He stirs the contents in the deep skillet again. "It's about ready. Do you mind grabbing the bread out of the oven? The mitts are in the drawer to the left of it."

"Sure."

"It's already cut. I put it in there to keep it warm. Why don't you take that and your wine to the table, I'll be right there with dinner."

"Okay," I agree, doing as he suggests.

I sit down at the long side of the table where we'll be closer. A few moments later he sets a white bowl down in front of me causing my mouth to water. The shells are removed from the pink shrimp, mixed in with the white of the orzo, and the greens and reds of the veggies, a picture perfect, colorful palette. "This looks amazing, Levi."

He smiles and strides back to the kitchen, retrieving his wine, butter, and some fresh parmesan before sitting down across from me. "Dig in," he urges, his eyes glued to me.

"Don't watch."

"What?" He laughs, but my eyes narrow. "Okay, fine. Just eat." He picks up his fork, flicking his gaze from me to his own food and back before taking a bite.

The moment my mouth closes over my fork, the flavors burst in my mouth and my eyes reflexively close. A soft hum escapes, as I savor the taste. "Oh my god, Levi, this is delicious."

"Thank you," he rasps, his voice strained. "But if you eat every bite like that, I may not make it through dinner."

My face flushes and my stomach twists. "Um, I'm ah...I'm sorry."

"Please, don't be sorry." His eyes glint with mischief.

I need to change the subject before I really start fumbling. "So, um, you're definitely much smoother than you were on our first date."

He quirks his brow. "Is that supposed to be a compliment?"

Feeling like we're getting back on even ground, I ask the question that's been circling, "For someone who can be all lines and ego, have you ever had a serious relationship, or have you always been a player?"

He flinches, but I'm not going to brush this question to the side. This is one answer I need to know.

Chapter 15

Levi

Frowning, my college girlfriend crosses my mind for the first time in years, the same woman I don't ever want to remember. I lift my glass to my lips, taking a gulp of wine. "You really want to jump right in tonight, huh?"

She shrugs, a look passing over her face before she swiftly shutters it. "It's just something I need to know."

With a firm nod, I finish my wine and look across the table at Layla, her eyes gentle, inviting. The look on her face has me opening my mouth and spilling truths I never thought I would to another woman. "I had a couple girlfriends in high school, but none of them were serious. Baseball and family kept me too busy for anything to last. My college girlfriend was a different story. I started dating her sophomore year and we were together until just before I got my contract with the Lions."

"What happened?" she asks, her voice timid.

"She never pressured me for my time, but we had fun when we were together. I tried to make things work with her and honestly, I thought she was the perfect girlfriend." I huff a laugh in contempt.

"But I was so fucking wrong," I grit through my teeth. Inhaling deeply and controlling my exhale, I attempt to pull myself together, hating the anxious look on Layla's face. "It's not what you're thinking."

She straightens. "I'm not thinking anything. I know better than to assume," she retorts, defensive.

Wincing, my stomach churns. "I'm sorry. But the men are always the bad guys right?" I scoff. "I think you can figure it out. The only difference is that I was the loyal one in our relationship. Heidi was the one who betrayed me. Apparently, she was cheating on me with a couple different guys from the football team at one point or another, waiting to see if one of us would go pro." My face scrunches up in disgust.

Her face turns sympathetic. "I'm sorry you went through that, Levi."

I shake my head. "It's fine. I'm glad I found out before it was too late. She's the last woman I really made an effort for and after that, I went pro and admittedly, I went a little wild. That's when I became the player you saw in the media. I was bitter and pissed off. Having a contract in the MLB made it so I didn't have to make any effort when it came to women. They didn't care who I was, just that I was signed and I sure as hell didn't want a commitment after that."

"I don't blame you."

Meeting her gaze, I see nothing but understanding. My only question is, how much? I hate the idea of her going through even a sliver of what I endured. "What about you? Might as well get it all out there now. Your exes?"

She snorts as if my question is funny. Her tanned skin heats and she quickly covers her mouth, but she doesn't need to. I already love that sound. "I had a couple boyfriends in college, but they were nothing to write home about."

"Did you ever date an athlete?"

She blushes, her eyes flitting to her food and reflexively back to me. "Um, yeah, I guess."

"What about a baseball player?" I push, my chest tightening, although I'm confident I already know the answer.

"Um, yeah," she whispers so quietly, I almost don't hear her admission.

"Did he cheat on you?" I question, not sure if she would tell me if I didn't ask directly. Her only response is a nearly imperceptible nod. My blood boils and my fists clench at my sides. "Who was he?"

"Gabe got in enough trouble when they got in a fight." She shakes her head. "I'm not telling you that."

"I could probably find out."

"Yeah, you could, but please don't. It doesn't matter. He doesn't matter."

"If he didn't matter, I might not be climbing such an uphill battle just to get you to go out with me."

She flinches. "I don't know if that's true or not, but I can tell you that it's more than just him. My father was the same kind of man." She slouches, her shoulders rounded, defeated while she plays with her food.

My chest tightens making it difficult to breathe. I can't imagine having to cope with a father like that as a little girl. The same men who is her role model for pro athletes, for baseball players. Even with her brother watching out for her, it would be hard not to judge. Heaving a sigh, I tell her, "I'm sorry, Layla."

"Don't be." She shakes her head dismissively. "I sure know how to ruin a date, huh?" she mutters under her breath.

My stomach twists seeing the heartbreak written on her face, urging me to do something for her. Reaching under the table, I find her knee and give it a tender squeeze. Waiting until she looks at me, I let a crooked grin take over my features. "Does that make us even?"

Another snort escapes her lips and we both burst out laughing. "I think that makes us friends," she claims, giving me a smile.

"We're much more than friends, Layla." I wink, only making her laugh harder. Damn, I love that sound, desperate to hear it again and again.

"You are an unabashed flirt, Levi Brennan. Even if you don't know what you're doing all the time." She's not able to hide her smile, letting me know she's teasing.

Arching my brow, my hand slides a little further up her silky skin, brushing the hem of her dress as I playfully challenge, "You want to test that theory?"

Her voice catches. "Um, no, I'm good."

My dick hardens and I lean back, clearing my throat. "Maybe we should eat dinner before we skip it all together?"

"I think that's a good idea."

She takes a sip of her wine before lifting her fork and savoring another bite of dinner. A small smile of satisfaction lights up my face. This woman is embedding herself into my world without even trying. My only reaction is to do everything I can for her, so she'll want to stay as much as I want her to be here.

Chapter 16

Layla

Leaning back against the counter, I watch the corded muscles on Levi ripple as he washes the dishes. "I really wish you'd let me help."

"I didn't invite you over to do my dishes."

"They're not just yours."

He tips his head, giving me an amused grin. "Do you ever let someone do something for you without asking questions or trying to help?"

Pursing my lips, I pretend to think about it. "Nope," I reply, popping the P.

He chuckles and turns off the water, turning to face me. "Thank you for coming over tonight," he sates, his voice low and gravelly shooting heat straight to my core. I could listen to him talk all night.

"Thanks for having me." Licking my lips, my eyes roam his toned form as he dries his hands and tosses the towel on the counter. "Why me?" I blurt out the question before I can think about it.

His mouth falls open, his movements staccato before becoming fluid again as he sidles towards me. "Are you seriously asking me that?" he asks, clearly perplexed.

My face heats, but I nod in affirmation. "Yes. Why me? You don't do relationships anymore and now I know why. After our shitty blind date, you could've forgotten about it, about me."

"I'd never forget about you," he interrupts. "And I sure as hell needed to apologize."

"Okay, so say you're sorry and go. But why are you all of a sudden willing to take a risk with someone you barely know? Why me, Levi?"

He holds my stare, his eyes intense, closing the distance until he's standing in front of me without making contact. His warm breath fans my face as he looks down at me until I avert my gaze, dropping it to his chest. My heart hammers against my ribcage, while I stare straight ahead, focusing on breathing.

Suddenly, his hands grip my waist, lifting me and making me squeal. I suck in a quick breath as he places me on the cool granite countertop. Planting his hands beside me and caging me in, he leans in close, so close I can't look at anything but him. "Why you? It may be only one question, but I have a million answers."

I gasp, my heart squeezing. "Levi," I whimper.

"I'll start with something simple. You're stunning, Layla."

Shaking my head, I argue, "You see beautiful women all the time."

"Not like you," he claims, his voice full of conviction. "When I walked through the door at the diner and saw you sitting alone, my mouth nearly hit the floor. The way your hair fell across your shoulders, I wanted to run my fingers through it to see if it was as soft as it looked." He gives a gentle tug of my ponytail, tipping my head back. "I wanted to brush my lips over your silky, tanned skin." His mouth skims down my neck eliciting goosebumps. "My fingers were itching to caress the sides of your breasts to see your nipples peak towards me." His knuckles skim my sides, my breasts heavy, my nipples pert, straining towards him. "You have this breathtaking body you hide behind a librarian image and it's sexy as fuck."

My entire body is on fire, my juices pooling in my panties. I'm desperate to pull my legs together for some friction, but it's impossible with him standing between them. Instead, I keep pushing him.

Breathily, I argue, "Those are not things that are unique to me."

"Yes, they are. Those things, *everything* about you is special Layla because you don't compare to anyone else I've ever laid eyes on." He presses a soft kiss to my jaw. "But I'm happy to give you more."

Gently, his tongue flicks out, licking a spot behind my ear, eliciting a soft moan. "Yes, please."

"I've never seen eyes so bright, and full of emotion, so expressive. I tried to block it out, but I couldn't. Even when I thought you were using me, I didn't want to walk away."

"You didn't. I did."

Leaning back, he looks into my eyes. "Which gives me another list of reasons I want you to stay. You don't put up with bullshit, you have a kind heart, and you mean what you say."

"A lot of people do," I interrupt.

"Not with me. But you know my world intimately and it doesn't matter to you. You're smart and stand your ground. You fight for what you want and what you believe in and that's part of what makes you absolutely stunning. Sure, you can be quiet, but you're fierce and letting you go could be deadly for me. You're not just the woman I want, you're exactly what I need. I want you, Layla. Every piece of you. Claws, fur, and all," he claims.

Before I can respond, his mouth drops, sealing his lips over mine. A soft moan escapes as I melt into him. His hands slide up my sides and cups my face, holding me to him. Moving together soft and slow, but also firm and unrelenting, I kiss him back. My hands snake into his hair and I gently haul him towards me when his tongue slips inside, tangling with mine.

One hand glides down my neck and side, landing on my thigh once again. His thumb rubs slow circles on my skin, inching up my leg. My breathing picks up its pace and I kiss him harder, almost frantic before my head falls back desperate for breath. His lips drop to my collarbone, licking, nibbling, sucking.

"I love the red against your skin," he mumbles, kissing me again.

Careful of his shoulder, my hands glide down, digging into his back. "My panties match," I reveal breathlessly.

"Fuck me," he mutters, his fingers crawling further up the inside of my thigh, my statement, his permission.

"Kiss me," I beg. His mouth finds mine once again, devouring me. His fingers sweep over my panties, enflaming my already burning core making me moan into his mouth.

The sound of a door opening and closing, followed by his aunt calling, "Levi? Are you here?"

Levi freezes and I launch myself off the kitchen counter, slipping between him and the granite with a yelp. He chuckles and answers, "We will be right out, Aunt Miranda."

Running my hands through my hair and over my dress, I spin around frantically as if I left something on the ground, but apparently it's only my dignity. "I'm so sorry."

"There's nothing to apologize for. Relax," he insists, pressing a kiss to my forehead. Linking our fingers, he guides me out to the living room.

His aunt's eyes widen when she sees me. "Oh, I'm so sorry to interrupt."

"Layla and I were just cleaning up dinner," he explains, grinning.

"Um, yeah." Flushed, I rush to escape, yanking my hand away. "I'm sorry, but I have to get going. Thank you for dinner, Levi."

"Let me walk you home."

"You don't have to do that."

"I want to," he insists.

"Okay." I agree. "It was good to see you Mrs. Brennan."

"Please, call me Miranda." I nod in affirmation. "And I'll see you at book club."

"Oh, yes. I'll be there."

I rush out the door with Levi close behind. He easily catches me just as the back gate closes, his arm falling over my shoulders and tugging me close. "You're in a rush to get out of there."

"I'm mortified," I emphasize, the heat rushing to my face once again.

Chuckling, he reminds me, "She was one of the women who set us up and we are more than old enough to be kissing."

"I know, but..." I scrunch my nose up and he laughs, pressing a kiss to the top of my head.

"You're adorable."

"Gee thanks," I mutter only making him laugh harder.

Moments later we walk up to my front door and I stop, his hand falling to his side as I turn to look at him. "Thank you for tonight. I had a lot of fun."

Reaching behind my head, he grips my ponytail and gently tugs until I meet his gaze. "Me too. Thank you for giving me a chance."

I lick my suddenly dry lips and push up on my tiptoes, while he lowers his head to meet me halfway. We're quickly lost in another kiss as he spins me, pressing me against my front door. His lips glide over mine, his taste, his touch igniting every piece of me. If I'm not careful, I may climb him like a tree right in front of my house.

Dragging myself out of my Levi induced haze, I place my hand on his chest, and give him a gentle nudge, halting his movements.

Both of us gasp for breath as he looks into my eyes, searching. "I think I need to take this slow."

"I'm just kissing you goodnight," he claims, his eyes sparkling with mischief and his smile devilish.

"Your lips feel like a helluva lot more than just a kiss goodnight."

He smirks. "Then, maybe I should try it again." He hesitates only a moment before seeing my assent in my eyes, pressing his lips to mine once again, eliciting a desperate sound from my mouth.

Lost in Levi, it takes me a moment to notice as the door behind me swings open and I fall back, a startled scream fleeing. Levi's arm tightens around my waist and he swiftly brings me flush to his body to keep me from tumbling. My eyes open, meeting my brother's narrowed gaze just over Levi's shoulders. "Hey, Sis. Have fun tonight?"

Levi stands me back on my feet keeping his hand on my back. I sway momentarily, giving a slight shake of my head. "What the hell, Gabe?" I demand the moment I get my bearings.

He chuckles, shrugging, his gaze veering to the man still holding me and watching me close. Levi holds out his free hand to my brother. "Levi Brennan."

Gabe crosses his arms over his chest and glares at Levi. I smack him in the arm. "Don't be an ass."

Sighing, he shakes Levi's hand. "Gabe, but you already know that."

Levi nods. "You have a great arm for a first baseman."

"And you have a shitty slider, but I don't mind."

Levi chuckles as their hands fall to their sides. "You're not wrong. It's not my best, especially this year."

"Thanks for bringing Layla home safe."

I scoff, but Levi laughs and acquiesces. "It's late. I'll see you tomorrow, Layla."

My eyebrows furrow, not recalling any plans. Leaning down, he brushes his lips over mine, with my brother unmoving, as if standing guard. Butterflies scatter around my belly and I blush a deep shade of red, but don't comment.

"Bye, Levi," I say, my voice quiet, unsure. "Thank you for tonight."

He waves and stuffs his hands in his pockets as he turns and strides away. Could this night be any more embarrassing?

"Nothing more than friends, huh?" Gabe asks, chuckling. Groaning, I trudge into the house after my brother.

Chapter 17

Levi

Grasping a bouquet of fall flowers in one hand and a bag of Mexican takeout in the other, I knock awkwardly on Layla's front door, trying not to damage the flowers. The door swings open, and Gabe stands in the doorway with a somewhat triumphant grin on his face, throwing me off.

"Well, look who's here," he announces. "How are you, Levi?"

"Hi, Gabe. Is Layla home?"

"You bring dinner and flowers and don't know if she's home?" He chuckles and takes a step back, gesturing for me to come inside. "Is there enough for me?"

"Yeah, there's plenty."

"Smart man," he states, patting me firmly on my back, just below my right shoulder blade.

Flinching, I mutter, "Watch the shoulder."

At my words, Layla jumps up from the couch and storms over to us, visible fury in her petite form. "What did you do?" she asks, glaring at Gabe.

"Nothing," he claims, holding up his hands as if he's innocent. "I'm sorry, Levi. I wasn't thinking."

"I'm fine, Layla. It wasn't intentional."

She side-eyes her brother making him chuckle. "Sure, it wasn't."

"It's okay," I insist.

Sighing, she brings her tired gaze back to me. "What are you doing here anyway?"

"I brought you dinner and some flowers." I hold the bouquet out for her, relishing the smile that lights up her face.

"Thank you. These are beautiful, but if you keep this up, I will run out of room for my stuff."

Grinning in response, I change the subject. "Do you like Mexican?"

"Yes, but, we didn't have plans tonight. What are you doing here, Levi?"

"Just say thank you, Layla and let the man into the kitchen," Gabe answers sounding exasperated.

I chuckle and arch my eyebrow in response, waiting for her to decide. Her appreciative smile is all I need, her cheeks tinging a deep shade of red.

"Thank you, Levi."

"I brought a little of everything since I wasn't sure what you would like and I knew Gabe was here too."

"If you don't want to date him, Layla, maybe I can convince him to date me," Gabe jokes. "Even if he is a Lion."

We all laugh. Layla steps closer to me and pushes up on her tiptoes, her hand resting on my forearm as she presses her lips to the corner of my mouth. My heartbeat skyrockets as she falls back on her heels. "Thank you."

A grin lights up my face. "You're welcome. I figured with adding me to your schedule, you have a busy week. I'm sure you're tired, so I wanted to do something for you."

"You didn't have to do that, but I do appreciate it."

"So do I," Gabe adds, smirking. "What did you bring?" He claps and rubs his hands together.

Layla laughs, playfully shoving her brother, but he doesn't move an inch. "What is wrong with you?"

I unpack the food, Layla sets it out on the counter and Gabe grabs plates, silverware, and drinks for all of us. After we fill our plates, and sit down at the table, I glance at Gabe. "Sorry about the end of your season."

Frowning, he replies, "Me too, but it wasn't as bad as the end of yours."

"Mine was over before the team, I just hope it's not permanent."

"You have the best helping you get in shape now. If anyone can get you there, it's Layla."

I glance between the two siblings. Their admiration, respect, and love for each other apparent. Gabe's faith in her shows how intelligent and skilled she truly is. "Why aren't you a physical therapist for a pro sports team? You have the resumé, the talent and the connections."

Gabe takes a bite of a burrito and arches his eyebrow in question, like me, waiting for his sister's response.

Her eyes flicker back and forth between us. "Um, I think you both know why. I haven't had the best experience with players."

"So, you're saying that you're letting dad and fuckface interfere with your dreams?" Gabe challenges, his tone filled with disbelief.

She shakes her head. "No, but why should I put myself in a situation where I know I'll be miserable."

Her brutal honesty feels like a punch to the gut, Gabe seeming to mirror my reaction.

"And my words obviously need repeating. You're too smart to be standing by the sidelines when you could be a real help. Not all players are like dad and Hurst," Gabe states, his voice soft, supportive.

"Hurst? Cal Hurst?" My mouth drops and my body stiffens, glancing at Layla. Her eyes go wide, looking from her brother to me and back.

"Shit, he didn't know," he mutters in understanding.

"Just not who," I grit through my teeth, my blood boiling and my fingers twitching. How could someone hurt her like that? Knowing who makes it feel more real and I hate that for her. She doesn't deserve it.

"I didn't let him get away with it," Gabe claims.

"You two both need to stay far away from him," Layla insists, likely knowing what's running through my head.

Gabe scoffs. "Kinda hard to do when he plays for the Mavericks. I'd give almost anything to get rid of him."

"Can we not talk about him anymore?" Layla requests, her voice pleading. "He's not worth it."

I scoff, grumbling under my breath, "You can say that again."

"Please?" The look she gives me makes my chest tight and I give her a nearly imperceptible nod.

"Have you checked to see what teams are looking for a new physical therapist? There's always some sport that's in their preseason or hiring," Gabe emphasizes.

"Not really," she answers, heaving a sigh. "What are your plans during the offseason, Gabe?" She glares at her brother.

"Okay, okay." He holds his hands up in surrender. "I get it."

Layla's cell phone rings and she looks down, her shoulders sagging as she answers it. "Hi, Mom."

Pausing, she glances at Gabe. "Okay, we'll be right over." She disconnects without another word.

"We?" Gabe questions, arching his brow.

"She fell. I need your help."

"Fuck me," Gabe mutters.

"Do you need my help?"

Layla shakes her head. "If I brought someone new with me when she's hurt, she'd likely disown me."

"Are you sure? I don't mind."

"No, thanks." Pushing up on her tiptoes, she forces a smile and presses a chaste kiss to my lips. "Thank you for the flowers and dinner...again."

"You're welcome. Call me if you need my help."

"I will. I'm going to change. Bye, Levi."

"Bye." My eyes follow after her, down the hall until she disappears into her bedroom on the left.

Gabe steps up next to me. "I'm not sure if you mentioned her job tonight to get my attention, but that's exactly what you did. I want you to know that I'm not letting either of those assholes hold her back from what she wants anymore." I nod in approval. "You're all right Brennan."

"I could say the same about you. See you later, Gabe."

"Thanks for dinner," he adds as I walk out the door, wishing there was more I could do to help.

My abrupt exit leaves me feeling oddly forlorn and helpless.

Chapter 18

Layla

"I'm here," Gabe says as more of a mantra, just before we walk in the front door at our mom's small ranch. Neither of us are sure what to expect, and we only hope she's okay.

Not able to speak, I reach out with my shaky hand and give his a squeeze, following him inside.

"Layla? Gabe? Is that you?" she calls. "I'm in the kitchen."

"Yeah, it's us, Mom. We're coming," Gabe answers for both of us.

We walk through the living room, Kleenex piled high on the coffee table next to cans of diet soda, empty water bottles and candy wrappers. We round the corner into the kitchen and my breath catches, an overwhelming stench fills our senses. I'm not sure if it's spoiled milk or if my mom had an accident while she was waiting for help. We spot her sprawled on the linoleum floor in a dirty blue nightgown with broken glass surrounding her and a chair tipped over, too far to reach.

"I'm so sorry to bother you two, but I slipped and couldn't get up. I wasn't sure who else to call."

My chest tightens and I struggle to breathe, wondering what she forgot to end up in this position and how long she waited before she called us. Fighting back my tears, I attempt to focus on the task at hand and force out words I hope will help calm all three of us. "It's okay, mom. I'm glad you had your phone close by to call us. We're here now."

Gabe steps towards her, the glass crunching beneath his shoes. He reaches over, lifting her as if she weighs nothing and carefully placing her back on her feet outside the mess. "Why don't you help mom get cleaned up and I'll take care of everything in here," he suggests.

I nod in agreement. "Thanks, Gabe."

He gives me a sad but encouraging smile.

For the next hour and a half, I zone out, doing what I need to do to help my mom, my heart aching more every second. She doesn't deserve this. No one does.

We finally tuck her into bed and climb into Gabe's truck to head home. He grips the steering wheel tight, his knuckles turning white. "You didn't tell me it had gotten this bad, Layla. It's not safe for her to be there alone anymore."

"She swore she was okay. I believed her. I thought she was doing better," I sob, tears streaming down my face. "She's way too young for this, Gabe."

"The disease doesn't give a fuck how old she is," he snaps.

Gasping, I flinch away from him, reflexively crowding the window.

Heaving a sigh, he immediately apologizes. "I'm sorry. I just feel so fucking helpless."

"Me too," I concede.

We drive a few minutes in silence and he finally asks, "Is mom the real reason you haven't searched for another job outside Love Canyon?"

My body sags in defeat. "Maybe. I don't know."

He turns into my driveway and shuts off the car. "I'm sorry you've been dealing with all of this alone."

"I know."

"We need to find her a place that can help her."

I gulp down the lump in my throat. "Can't we take turns helping her while you're home? Like doing errands for her and checking on her more?"

"Sure, we can, but what about when I go back? You can't do this by yourself anymore, Layla."

A defeated sigh falls from my lips. "I know."

"We'll start tomorrow."

I nod my head robotically. "Okay."

"You know there's a good chance that we won't find anything around here for mom."

"Yeah."

He gives me a look. "Maybe we should consider looking for something closer to me in Oregon. You could find a great job out there if you wanted."

My chest tightens with both fear and anticipation. After coming back, I almost wondered if I would leave again, but having my mom safe and close to both Gabe and me is ideal. The thought of Levi flickers through my mind, but I swiftly shove it away, questioning my sanity. My family needs to be my priority. Levi and I are barely finding our footing, and he'll be leaving to go back to Vegas in a few months without me anyway. "You're probably right."

Taking a deep breath, I look at my brother with tears in my eyes. "I'm really glad you're here, Gabe."

Leaning over, he wraps me in his arms, hugging me and I squeeze him back. "I love you, Layla."

"Love you, too."

"Are you going to be okay tonight?"

Not really, but there's no point in admitting it. "Yeah, I'll be fine."

We climb out of the car and drag ourselves inside. "I'm jumping in the shower and then I'm going to go out for a drink."

"You're walking?"

"Yes, I promise."

"Okay, I'll see you in the morning."

Trudging to my room, I clean up, changing into a thin pair of black and white pajama pants and a black tank top. Grabbing my phone, I send a quick text to work, letting them know that I'm not feeling well and won't make it in tomorrow. The moment I sit down on the edge of my bed, I jump up, antsy, on edge. "I can't stay here right now," I mumble under my breath.

Slipping on a pair of shoes and a thin purple zip up, I grab my keys, phone and purse and start walking, my concern for my mom overwhelming. A few minutes later, I find myself standing in front of Levi's house, burdened with indecision and maybe a little bit of guilt. He shouldn't be the one I turn to, not when neither of us can stay. I should go. Shifting awkwardly back and forth, I decide to take a chance, not wanting to be alone. I slip into the backyard and tiptoe to Levi's door, knocking softly, with my heart pounding like I'm doing something wrong.

Just when I'm about to give up, the door opens, and a bare chested Levi stands in front of me in nothing but navy blue boxer shorts making me gasp. The hard ridges of his chest and abs leave my throat dry. I drag my eyes up to his, finding him looking down at me with a sleepy but concerned gaze, his hair in sexy disarray. "Layla," he rasps, his voice low, rolling over me like velvet. "Are you okay?"

I nod, spikes erupting on the inside of my throat, while tears quickly well in my eyes. "Yeah," I rasp, fighting to keep my lower lip from trembling. "I'm sorry I woke you up."

Reaching for me, he wraps his hand around my arm, and soothingly tugs me inside, shutting the door behind me. Without a word, he entwines our fingers and squeezes, a shock of heat rushing through me, warming me like a blanket. Gently, he guides me towards his bedroom, his presence alone, soothing. Still holding my hand, he sits down on his bed, watching me, waiting for me to speak, but I can't. Not yet.

Gently, I twist my hand away, slipping off my coat and shoes, and discarding them on the floor before crawling into his bed without an invitation.

Sighing softly, he lays down next to me and gathers me into his chest, holding me tight. Tears spill over onto his skin, and he tucks me closer, rubbing reassuring circles on my back. Breaking the silence, he repeats his earlier question. "Layla, I'm happy to hold you all damn night and even longer if you'll let me, but first, I need to know, are you okay?"

Instead of answering, I explain, "My mom has early onset dementia." My admission squeezes my insides in a vice grip.

"I'm so sorry," he whispers, pressing kisses to the top of my head as he brings me impossibly closer.

"Thank you," I whimper, barely getting the words out. There's nothing else to say, but his whispered words of regret and comfort calm me. Settling into his warm embrace, and inhaling his clean, woodsy scent, my tears eventually diminish as I drift off to sleep encased in his heartening presence.

Chapter 19

Levi

The weight of Layla's warm body presses up against me, my dick stiff and uncomfortable not getting the memo that she's not here for sex. I'd been about to fall asleep when I heard the quiet knocking, but when I dragged my tired limbs to the door, I was pleasantly surprised until I got a good look at her face, and my heart plummeted. She stood in front of me appearing frail, exposed and defenseless. My need to hold her and comfort her nearly consumed my insides. I'm grateful she let me.

I can't imagine what she's going through. Her confession floored me, showing her strength even in this moment of vulnerability, making her even more beautiful. Knowing I'm the one she sought out when she needed someone to lean on fills me with pride, but I don't want to take it for granted. I want to prove to her that I'm a man who deserves to be by her side through thick and thin.

At the same time the thought crosses my mind, I'm overwhelmed with the truth of it. Layla has quickly and easily embedded herself into my heart whether she meant to or not. And for the first time in a long damn time, I don't want to let her slip away.

Pressing my lips to the top of her head, I'm hit with the soft scent of vanilla and lavender bringing a smile to my face. My hand slowly trails over her silky smooth tresses onto her back, her body curling into mine, fitting perfectly.

She shifts underneath me and I still, waiting. Slowly, she lifts her head and turns towards me, her eyes fluttering open, her brown orbs focusing on me. Her tongue flicks out, licking her lips and she rasps, "Hi."

A grin covers my face. "Good morning, beautiful. How are you feeling?"

Planting her palm on my bare chest, she pushes up and looks down at me. My hand covers hers, keeping her there. "Um, I'm okay. I'm sorry for waking you up last night."

Giving her hand a squeeze, I keep my voice low, but insistent, "You can wake me up anytime you need me. I'm happy I could be there for you last night and I want to be there for you while you go through this. It can't be an easy road."

She stares at me as if trying to read me and hopefully sees the truth in my eyes before she finally responds. "Thank you, Levi. I can't begin to explain how much that means to me." She sits up fully and I release her hand, following suit. "Last night, I don't know. I just couldn't be at home and I started walking. Without thinking, I ended up here."

"I'm glad you came to me, Layla, but next time call me and I'll come to pick you up. Yes, Love Canyon is a small town, but you never know what could happen. It's not safe to be walking alone so late at night."

She rolls her eyes, teasing, "Yes, sir."

A salacious grin lights up my face. "Oh, I could definitely get used to hearing that come out of your mouth."

"Levi," she scolds, blushing a deep shade of red.

Relishing her reaction, I chuckle. Giving her a reprieve, I glance at the time. "You don't have to work today, do you? Otherwise, you're late."

Shaking her head, she states, "No, I called in last night."

"So does that mean I have the entire day with you?"

"Umm…"

"Just say, yes. I want to take care of you today."

"I feel like you've already been doing that."

"Please?" Arching my brows, I give her a crooked grin that I know usually helps me get my way.

Sighing, she relents, "Okay, but let's say we're spending the day together. You don't have to take care of me."

"I'll concede if you let me do some things for you."

"Why is this a negotiation?" She laughs, the sweet sound sending tingles down my spine. "Fine, but I have to go check on my mom later. You don't have to come with me for that."

"Would you like me to?"

She opens her mouth, hesitating. "It's just that I don't want you to have to do that. She might be fine, but I can't promise anything."

"Well, then if it's okay, I'd like to go with you."

Her eyes widen and a look stretches across her face, I can't quite decipher but it elicits a warm rush of waves cresting deep in my gut. Nodding, she whispers, "Yeah, I would like that."

Leaning towards her, I brush my lips over hers and pull back, looking into her eyes. "Are you hungry? Would you like some breakfast?"

Her stomach grumbles in response, both of us chuckling. "That means yes, but you have to let me help you cook this time."

I press my lips to hers once again and climb out of bed. Holding my hand out for Layla, I wait until she takes it. Scrambling out of bed, she follows me into the kitchen. "What would you like to eat?"

"I make really good French toast and scrambled eggs," she offers.

"As long as we cook together, it sounds delicious."

She smiles at me causing my chest to tighten. My fingers itch to reach for her. Turning away before I lift her onto the countertop and devour her, I start grabbing all the pans and food we need.

"Levi?"

Halting, I spin around and look at her, staring at me, nibbling on her lower lip making my dick twitch. Arching a brow, I struggle to keep my voice steady as I prod, "Yes?"

Releasing her lip, she ambles towards me, tipping her head back to look up at me the closer she gets. Stopping right in front of me, she places her palm on my chest eliciting goosebumps and takes a deep breath as if for courage. "Thank you." My eyes widen and my stomach twists. This woman. "Thank you for being there for me and for being exactly what I needed when even I didn't know what that would look like."

Her words feel like she just reached inside my chest and claimed my heart, squeezing it in the palm of her hand, in tune with every heartbeat.

Sliding my hands up her sides, I cradle her face in my hands, staring into her eyes. "It's exactly where I want to be." Closing the distance between us, I press my lips to hers. Our mouths move together, slow and tender, tingles spreading throughout my body as it ignites the spark between us. Tilting my head, I deepen our kiss. Her mouth opens on a soft moan, spurring my desire and inviting me in. My fingers thread into her hair, holding her close. I groan as my tongue juts out, tasting, licking, exploring, getting lost in our kiss, in her.

"Levi?" Aunt Miranda calls from the living room, breaking our moment. Layla swiftly tears our mouths apart.

"Shit. I didn't even hear her come in," I mutter under my breath. Layla giggles and I back away, responding to my aunt. "In the kitchen Aunt Miranda."

I hear the sound of her footsteps approaching as I set a pan on the stove. Her eyes widen, and a smile lights up her face the moment she spots Layla opening the bread. "Layla! I didn't realize you were here. I'm sorry to intrude."

Layla's cheeks are red, but she schools her expression. "Hi, Mrs. Brennan. Levi and I are just making breakfast. Are you hungry?"

She laughs. "Oh, no, dear. I was just stopping in to see if my nephew had eaten yet, but it looks like the two of you have everything covered. I'm headed into town to get some groceries. Do you need anything?"

"No, thank you," I reply. "You really spoil me, Aunt Miranda."

She presses her lips together and waves off my comment. "I'll see you later. You two have fun."

"Bye," we both call as she leaves.

Layla sags against the counter and both of us burst out laughing. "It almost feels like being a teenager again," I joke.

She makes a face. "Not for me, but I get it."

"What do you mean, not for you? You never made out with anyone on your living room couch afraid you would be caught?"

Frowning, she shakes her head. "Nope. No boyfriend until college, remember?"

"And you grew up here? The boys at your school were idiots."

"Not going to argue with you there," she mutters, "but probably not for the same reasons." She shakes her head. "Let's not talk about them. I'd much rather focus on the man in this kitchen."

"I'll go along with that," I say, giving her a chaste kiss. I could get used to having her in my kitchen.

"I'm sure you will." She laughs, the sound light again, bringing a smile to my face. "After breakfast settles, we should do your PT."

"You're right. Then, we'll have the rest of the day to do as we please." Stepping up to her, I move our bodies flush, my front to her back and press a kiss behind her ear.

A low hum falls from her mouth. "Mmm…" She stands a little straighter and suggests, "How about I make the French toast and you make the eggs?"

"Sounds like a plan." I grab the eggs out of the refrigerator and steal another glance at Layla as she takes a hairband off her wrist and rakes her fingers through her hair, tying it up in a high ponytail before she moves any further. The simple action draws my attention back to her delectable neck and I force myself to look away or we'll never eat.

Chapter 20

Layla

I fidget in the passenger seat of Levi's car on the short drive to my mom's. Levi is meeting my mom. I repeat the words in my head, not quite believing it. If someone asked me how this happened I wouldn't be able to answer. Are we even dating? It doesn't matter. He's here and I'm nervous as hell. This isn't about Levi meeting my mom. It's about having no idea what we're walking into. I only hope today is one of her good days.

"Are you okay?" Levi asks glancing at me out of the corner of his eye. "Layla?" he prods when I remain silent. Reaching across the seat, he gives my knee a gentle squeeze in support.

"Yeah, sorry. I'm okay."

He sighs, parking his car in front of the small white ranch I grew up in. "Are you sure you want me to come inside?"

Turning my head to face him, I insist, "Yes, I'm sure. I'm just anxious about what she will be like, especially after last night. I promise, this has absolutely nothing to do with you."

"I'm not going to judge her, or you. That's not me."

"I don't think you are." Taking a deep breath, I say, "Okay, let's go." I climb out of the car and stride up the walkway with Levi right behind me. Not stopping, I push in the front door and step inside.

My gaze travels over the cozy living room with a small tan floral couch, a chocolate brown recliner and the tables now clear of the Kleenex and empty bottles and cans Gabe and I cleaned up last night. I breathe a sigh of relief knowing it didn't revert to the mess overnight.

"Mom?" I call, hesitant.

"Layla? I'll be right out," she replies.

"Okay. I brought someone with me," I add, hoping she doesn't walk out in her nightgown or something.

He glances around the room, noticing my senior picture with me dressed in a black dress alongside my brother's in a black suit. "You were beautiful then too," he says, grinning. Just below that, is my kindergarten graduation picture, my two front teeth missing from my smile. "That one is too cute."

I arch my eyebrow, blushing. "Thanks."

My mom steps into the room dressed in black pants and a simple dark red, long-sleeved top bringing a smile to my face. Exhaling, my shoulders truly relax seeing the mom I know. "Hi, Layla."

"Hi, Mom." Happy, I step towards her and give her a hug. "How are you feeling today?"

"I'm so much better. Thank you for helping." I nod in acknowledgement. "Who's this handsome young man?" she asks sounding older than her 59 years.

"Oh, sorry. This is my...um, this is Levi."

Levi grins and steps up to my mom, holding out his hand in greeting. "It's wonderful meeting you. I've heard so much about you."

She smiles and takes his hand, squeezing instead of shaking it and making me blush. "It's wonderful to meet you too, Levi. You must be special because Layla doesn't bring many boys around here."

"Mom!" I interrupt.

My mom chuckles, attempting to brush it off, while my face is completely on fire with embarrassment. "Oh, don't be so uptight, Layla. It's fine. I'm just happy to meet the man."

Levi's eyes sparkle, his grin wider. "I'm happy to be here," Levi reiterates, glancing at me.

"Why don't you two have a seat, stay for a little while. I made a cheese board if you would like some snacks. I could go get that for you."

I shake my head. "No, thank you, Mom. We're okay. We just ate, but we'll stay and talk for a little while."

"Okay," she agrees. My eyes remain on her until she sits down in the recliner. Making my way over to the couch, I sit down, Levi lowering himself down, right next to me. "I just hung up with your brother a few minutes ago. He wants to pick me up and take me to visit a couple of those homes on Monday."

"Don't you think that's a good idea? Some of them are really nice. Gabe sent me the ones he wanted to bring you to check out."

She presses her lips together. "Hmm." Looking around, she leans forward as if about to tell us a secret. "Yeah, but I'll be the youngest one at any of them. I don't want you and Gabe to have to worry anymore."

"We just want you to be safe, Mom."

Nodding, she turns to Levi. "So, you're the one that went out on a blind date with Layla. I thought you weren't very nice."

My face heats and Levi's head falls back as he bursts out laughing. "Thanks a lot, Mom," I mutter under my breath.

Levi catches his breath and says, "It's okay. We know it's true, but I begged her for forgiveness. A lot of apologizing, a few bouquets of flowers and some dinners, I think I might finally be getting her to forgive me."

Mom narrows her eyes in warning at Levi. "Make sure you treat her right. No more of your nonsense."

He laughs again, his eyes bright with amusement. "That's my plan. She deserves all good things."

"You got that right," my mom agrees.

"Can we stop talking about this as if I'm not here?" I squeak, not able to even glance in Levi's direction.

He reaches for my hand and weaves our fingers together, but I still can't look at him. "Gabe told me that you play baseball."

"Yes, I do. Well, right now Layla's helping me with an injury. I hurt my shoulder and my elbow this season."

"Well, you have the best physical therapist there is. You should be playing again in no time."

"Thanks, Mom."

"Where are you from, Levi?"

"Originally, not too far from here. I'm staying with my Uncle Steve and Aunt Miranda. While I'm here."

"Oh, I know your family. I've met your dad before too when he was visiting his brother."

Levi frowns, his body briefly goes taut and he nods. "Yup. He's visited a few times."

I feel the tension suddenly radiating off him, his hand reflexively tightening its grip on mine. Tilting my head in his direction, I whisper, "Are you okay?"

He nods, forcing a smile. His phone rings and without looking at the screen, he jumps up. "I'm sorry I have to get this." With his phone in hand, he rushes out the front door.

"Hmm. He seems nice."

"Mom," I mumble in warning.

"Just make sure you know all his secrets before you decide to make a commitment. The good looking ones are always hiding something and I think he just proved it."

I heave a sigh. There's no point in arguing, but I have a feeling it has something to do with his dad. Hopefully he'll open up to me sooner or later. "I'm sorry, Mom, but we have to go. I have some paperwork I have to do since I missed work today."

She flinches knowing she was the reason. "Oh, okay. Well, thanks for stopping and tell Levi it was nice meeting him."

"I will." Strolling over to her, I give her a kiss on the cheek. "I love you, Mom."

"I love you too, sweetheart."

Waving, I walk out the door, finding Levi leaning against the passenger door of his car. He lifts his gaze, meeting mine and pushes off the metal. "I was just coming back inside."

Shaking my head, I mutter, "It's okay, Levi. I told her we had to go."

"I'm sorry."

"Don't apologize," I insist, climbing in the car.

He slides in behind the wheel and looks at me. "I'm not hiding anything, Layla," he claims as if reading my mind.

"It's fine."

"No, it's not." He pauses, running his hand through his hair. "It's just that my dad is an asshole."

"Believe me, I get it," I emphasize before heaving a sigh and dropping my gaze, feeling drained, defeated. It feels like he knows almost everything about me, but so much of him is still a mystery to me.

How is that a relationship? "I'm here to listen if you want."

"Yeah, I would like that, but I just can't right now." His claim feels like he's closing me out. Am I like the other women he dates? My gut wrenches, but I ignore it, his heavy questioning stare boring into me. "Do you want to maybe go to a movie? I don't remember the last time I'd been to one."

"Um, maybe next time. Since we already did your therapy earlier, I think I need to go home and get some work done. I'm behind on paperwork since I called in today."

His face falls and he leans back against the seat, starting the car. "Okay. I understand."

Chapter 21

Levi

The look on Layla's face when I wasn't ready to talk last night hits me like a punch every time it crosses my mind. I saw her eyes shutter as if I betrayed her and close down just before she walked away. My gut told me not to let her go, but my head didn't catch up fast enough and now I'm paying for it.

My cell rings causing my heart to lurch, in hopes that it's Layla.

No such luck. Brady Williams, a friend from baseball camp when we were in high school lights up the screen. Trying to push aside my disappointment, I swipe to answer the call. "Brady, how the hell have you been?"

"Hey, Levi. I thought I'd give you a call to see how you're doing now that things seem to have settled down from the season."

"Yeah, as much as they can anyway." I laugh. "I'm all right. I escaped Las Vegas, at least for a while."

"I'm sure it's good to get out of there. How's the arm?"

"Not you too," I groan making him chuckle. "But I'll be honest with you, it's been okay. I just started working with a new physical therapist and she works wonders. I'm improving every day. How's Sam?" I ask about his girlfriend.

The smile in his voice is obvious when he answers, "She's good. She's my fiancé now. It's the other reason I called you. I'm engaged."

"Wow. Congratulations, Brady. That's fantastic news."

"Thanks. I'm really happy. So, what about you? Dating anyone besides what I've been seeing in the media?"

My heart drops into the pit of my stomach. "What do you mean? What did you see in the media, Brady? Shit. They better leave her the fuck alone."

"Whoa, Levi." He chuckles, talking me down. "It's okay. I've only seen some of the same old bullshit of you with a different woman every time and all of them claiming to be the love of your life."

I breathe a sigh of relief, my entire body sinking into the couch. "Thank fuck," I mutter under my breath.

"But you're obviously not talking about the same thing or same woman as me, so care to enlighten me?"

Frowning, I mutter, "I'd rather not."

"I promise the only one I'll share with is Samantha, but after that, you have to tell me. And you know I don't give a damn what they say in the news. You deserve to find some happiness."

"Fine, yeah, you're right. I met someone."

"About damn time. Tell me about her. How'd you meet?"

Chuckling, I admit, "I fucked up at first because I thought she was a cleat chaser, but I've been trying to make it up to her. She's damn gorgeous, smart as hell, and she knows baseball." The pride in my voice is obvious.

"So how do you know she's not a cleat chaser?"

"You know Gabe Romano?"

"Yeah, from the Mavericks, right? He's a fantastic first baseman."

"That's him. Layla is his sister."

"Oh, shit."

"Exactly. Anyway, I've been trying to get her to forgive me for being an ass when we first met, and I think she has, but I also feel like her walls are up. I'm trying to find a way to get through."

"You really do care about her," he mumbles in disbelief.

"Of course, I do, or you wouldn't even know her name."

He laughs in response. "Just saying, it's good to hear."

"Thanks. Any ideas on how I can show her I care?"

"Honestly, that's an individual question. With Sam, it was all about paying attention to what she needed or wanted from me. I fucked up too, but not intentionally. No one is perfect, Levi, just be smart and remember to always consider her. If she's worth it to you, go all in. Listen to her."

"Sounds simple enough."

Brady laughs. "Nothing is simple if you love her."

"Whoa. I didn't say anything about love. I'm interested. I like spending time with her and I think about her all the damn time, but it's too soon to be in love with this woman. It's barely been a week."

"And it's been over five years since you've had any interest in a woman besides getting them into your bed. I'm pretty sure it can happen faster than you expect. It did for me."

Running my hand through my hair, my heart pounds against my ribcage like a jackhammer at the idea of being in love. It's the first time I thought of love and haven't wanted to punch something at the mere concept. Maybe that's a possibility with Layla, but I would have to get her to agree to see more of me beyond her appointments to treat me. She can't keep pushing me away or our chance will be over before it begins. Spending time with her is exactly what I'm hoping for. I want more of everything when it comes to her. But does she feel the same? I crave everything about her.

"Levi? Did I lose you?"

"Sorry, Brady, I'm here."

"You okay?"

"Yeah, I just have a lot on my mind. But I need to go. I have something I've got to do."

"Okay. Take care of your arm. Sam and I want to come to a game next season and we'd like to see you on the field."

"I will. Thanks Brady. Tell Sam I said hi and congratulations," I say and end the call.

My mind races, thinking about the things I've already learned about Layla and connecting them to something special I could do for her, or something we could do together. Hopefully spending time with her will convert to her giving me a real chance.

An idea forms in my head. Turning towards the door, I stride to the main house, calling, "Aunt Miranda?"

Chapter 22

Layla

Dressed in black leggings and a pale pink, off the shoulder, short-sleeved sweater, I walk next to my best friend towards town. "I don't know what to do, Chloe, it just feels like it's moving so fast," I say, redoing my ponytail. "I went from not ever wanting to see the man again to going out with him again and again. Giving him a chance is just opening up the door for feelings. Isn't that irresponsible?"

She scoffs, arching her brow. "Really, Layla?"

Halting my footsteps, I spin and look at her. "He met my mother, Chloe. My mother," I say, emphasizing each word.

She chuckles. "You're making it sound like it's a bad thing. But to me, I think he's exactly the kind of book boyfriend you needed whether you realize it or not."

My eyes narrow at her. "Aren't you supposed to be on my side?"

"I am always one hundred percent team Layla and you know it. Liking someone, even a baseball player, is not the end of the world."

"Ugh. It's like you read my mind."

She laughs and I shake my head, fighting my own smile. Being around Chloe tends to lift my spirits, no matter my mood.

My phone vibrates in my pocket and I slip it out glancing at the screen. Levi calling.

"Is that him?" she asks.

"Yeah." I make a face and send him to voicemail, typing out a quick message.

> I'm on my way to book club with Chloe. I'll text you later.

I quickly slip my phone back in my pocket before I read the response I know is coming. It's better if I ignore it for now.

"You're going to have to talk to him and tell him how you're feeling. Avoidance is not an option."

I quirk a brow. "Evading was something the FMC in this week's book did well. Why can't that be me?"

"And how did that work out for her?" she questions, sarcasm thick on her tongue.

"You'd know if you read the book."

She shrugs like it's no big deal. "I didn't have any time this week. Beck and I had plans."

I nod, sighing. "Well, she made out damn well if you ask me. She even got the man in the end. That was after a lot of chaos, but it still worked out."

"Sounds like a raving endorsement." She laughs. "And what do you want Layla? Do you want the man?"

My face heats and my insides twist, a storm brewing. Hell, yes, is exactly what I want to say, but how can that be right? Having him inch into my life feels like a lot. Technically, I didn't only let him in, but I led the way, so I realize I'm not being fair. Unfortunately, my irrational panic doesn't give a damn.

"I want to be happy." She gives me a look as we step inside the bookstore. "Ugh, fine. Yes, I want him. How can I not? But I don't want to worry that he'll get bored with me, that I won't be enough, or that I'll give him my heart just for him to obliterate it and walk away."

Her eyes soften, her arm going protectively around my shoulders, guiding me towards the space at the back of the store. "That wouldn't happen, but if it did, he was not the right man for you in the first place."

Nodding, I gulp down the lump in my throat. "I'm scared to let go, Chloe, and if I do, there's no guarantee he won't be just like my father."

"Is that what's holding you back?" The sound of Levi's voice reverberates in my ears, my face heating, and my heart thumping.

Spinning on my heel, I come face to face with Levi, dressed in dark blue jeans and a black t-shirt, his simple threads making my heart race with the way they hang from his hard form. "What are you doing here?" I ask, breathlessly, barely able to hear my own voice over the blood pumping through my veins.

"I came here to see you," he confesses without preamble. "You're not exactly ghosting me, but it's still a brush off and I don't want that with you."

"Levi," I begin, but trail off, unsure of what I want to say. He's right.

"I should let you two talk," Chloe begins, her arm falling from my shoulders as she takes a step back.

"No!" I retort, grabbing her wrist as if my life depended on keeping her by my side. Her eyes widen, but she doesn't move.

"I'm sorry, Layla," Levi blurts out, taking another step towards me.

My eyebrows draw down in confusion. "Why are you apologizing?"

"Because I'm the one who didn't want to talk the other night after you opened up. You were vulnerable with me, but I couldn't reciprocate. It had nothing to do with you. I promise."

"It doesn't matter." I shake my head, attempting to dismiss him.

"Yes, it does. I'm used to closing myself off with other people when it comes to my father. He's not someone I talk about to anyone, ever," he emphasizes.

"It's fine, Levi. You don't have to tell me anything about him. It's not like you owe me."

"Telling you anything about me is not me returning a favor. What I share with you is because I care about you and I want you to know."

"I'm gonna go say hi to Scotty," Chloe mumbles, carefully yanking her hand away from me.

My eyes flash. "Wait. I'm sorry. Let me introduce you. Chloe, this is Levi. Levi, this is my best friend, Chloe."

He grins wide, shaking her hand as I reluctantly let her go. "It's nice finally meeting you, Chloe."

"You too, hot shot." She releases his hand and looks at me, arching her brow.

"Hot shot?" he questions, smirking.

"Book club is about to start, we should get our wine," I interrupt, striding for the bar without looking back, his answering chuckle giving me goosebumps.

Grabbing a glass of Moscato, I close my eyes, taking a large gulp. Opening my eyes, I finally realize Chloe and Levi are still chatting and I turn back to them.

"Come on, let's go sit down," I urge, tugging on Chloe's arm as she reaches for her own glass of wine.

The moment we sit, Levi takes the seat right next to me. Looking at him, I repeat my earlier question, "What are you doing here?"

"I wanted to spend time with you, so I thought I'd join your book club and I have to admit, this looks like a lot more fun than I expected."

"Levi–" I begin, but I'm immediately interrupted.

"Okay, everyone ready to dive into this week's book boyfriend?" Clara questions, attempting to get everyone's attention.

Laughter erupts around the room, thoughts already turning dirty. My face heats instantly, feeling Levi's eyes on me. Even with my olive skin, I'm pretty sure everyone in this room can tell I'm as red as a cherry tomato.

"Definitely a lot more fun," he whispers in my ear, making my hair stand on end and desire shoot straight through me making me squirm.

"Damn you, Levi Brennan," I mumble under my breath, his low, sexy chuckle his only response.

I'm so screwed.

Chapter 23

Levi

Walking out of book club with Layla, and Chloe, I can't wipe the smile from my face. It's obvious I'm getting to her in the best possible way and I'm enjoying every minute of seeing her squirm, pretending she doesn't feel anything when it comes to me.

"Why don't we go on a double date?" Chloe suggests. My grin grows as Layla narrows her eyes at her best friend. Maybe I'm not completely alone in this. "We could go ax throwing. I've heard that place is a lot of fun and Beck and I haven't been there yet."

My grin falls. Then again, maybe I'm already alone on the deserted island. "I think we should keep Layla away from ax throwing until I'm sure she's really willing to forgive me."

Layla snorts, her hand covering her mouth as her face heats. I'm truly growing to love that sound. It's carefree, beautiful. "Might be waiting a while," she mutters, playful, glancing at me out of the corner of her eye.

"I'll wait as long as you need," I whisper close to her ear, relishing in the goosebumps popping up on her skin.

"Fine. What about dinner?" Chloe urges.

"We're in," I agree, hoping she won't argue.

"I didn't–" she starts.

"Okay, great," Chloe interrupts, giving Layla a quick hug. "I'll see you later and we will hash out the details. I have to head home." Glancing at me she adds, "It was nice meeting you." Spinning on her heel, she waves without looking back.

"I like her," I declare.

"You would." Layla glares at me. "She has an opening for best friend if you want it."

Chuckling, I murmur, "Maybe she has good intuition and you could give me a chance."

"That's what I'm doing."

"Then, why have you been avoiding me?"

"You're the one who doesn't truly want to know me. If you did, you would also give me a piece of you." My brows scrunch together, puzzled, but she continues, "I've been giving you nearly the whole puzzle, even the things about my life that are hard. Yet, I still don't know any of the real stuff about you."

"Playing baseball isn't real?"

Tilting her head her eyes narrow, unimpressed by my sarcasm. "You know what I mean. Everyone knows you're a baseball player. I'm talking about things that make you Levi that the world doesn't know. Not necessarily secrets. Just things that are genuinely you."

"I told you I wanted to talk to you, Layla, and I meant it. I just needed a little time."

"And I can't be the only open one in our relationship. It's lonely and it's hard for me too."

Nodding, I tell her, "You're right and I'm sorry. I knew it as soon as you walked away, but I'm ready now."

She gives me a look, letting me know she's not sure if she should believe me, but my past is my only reason to hold back while everything else is screaming at me to give her my trust. "What are you saying, Levi?"

"I'm saying that I like you, Layla," I confess, my voice cracking on her name as if I were a teenage boy. "You're nothing like any other woman," I insist, desperate for her to see the truth in my eyes. "And I want to spend more time with you, for as long as you'll let me."

Gulping, she nods, holding my gaze. "Okay. I like you, too, Levi, but I'm not someone who can just date someone halfway. It's part of the reason why I questioned it when they put the two of us together on a blind date. Their success rate is hit or miss, so I wouldn't be surprised, but I really do like you."

I laugh. "They're batting average may be low, but I think with me and you, they hit this one out of the park."

She snorts, her head falling back as she bursts out laughing. "Now that was the line of a player."

Although it may have sounded like a line, it's true, but I don't bother repeating myself. Instead, I emphasize, "Former player."

She smiles, squeezing my heart. "Okay, Levi. But I need you to know, the moment I feel like you're keeping something from me or you don't talk to me, that's when I have the urge to walk away. My father was a man who held onto secrets like it was his duty. He built an armor around him, isolating himself, his family be damned. I refuse to ever live like that again for anyone, especially a man."

"Got it." Reaching for her hand, I thread my fingers through hers. "Would you like to go for a walk?"

She nods. "It's a nice night."

We stroll through town, my nerves haywire. Taking a turn, we approach the baseball fields at the edge of town. "My brother used to play Little League here. Thinking of where he is now, it's surreal."

"Believe it or not, I never played Little League," I admit.

She gasps. "Seriously?"

"Yeah. My dad wanted me to play football. He said baseball was for pussies."

Her eyes flare. "That's not true."

"I know, but as a kid..." I trail off, shrugging. Stepping forward, I drop her hand and lean against the chain link fence, looking out at the worn paint of the diamond on the dirt.

Her hand falls to my back in support, but she remains silent, waiting for me to continue. "I would sneak out to the fields and play with my friends, lying about where I'd been. Eventually, he caught on. I'll never forget the second I knew it was over. He showed up at the fields and glared at me. I was pitching and pretended like I didn't see him. Focusing on the game, I kept throwing, striking out everyone. The pride I felt barely lasted a moment. By the time my teammates were slapping me on the back, I wanted to run. I trudged towards him, feeling like I was marching to a death sentence. He stood with his arms crossed next to the dugout, glaring at every one of my friends that walked by him as if it was their fault I was there."

I shake my head, disgusted at the memory running through my mind. "As soon as I was within reach, he grabbed my pitching arm and dragged me home, dislocating my shoulder in the process." Layla's soft gasp rings in my ears. "He beat the shit out of me that night."

Layla slides her hand down my back and around my waist, her other hand mirroring the movements. Her head falls to my back, her body pressing in close as she squeezes me. "I'm so sorry, Levi," she says, her voice barely audible.

"He never laid a hand on me again."

"Once is too many times," she whispers so quietly, I almost don't hear.

Ignoring her comment, I push forward, or I'll never finish. "After that, my aunt and uncle helped me pay for my baseball camps and training far away from my dad, so anytime I was on break, I was nowhere near home and he could pretend like I didn't exist. They never knew the entire truth, but they suspected, especially when I begged them to help me get as far away from home as possible." I exhale harshly, my breath heavy, weighted with my confession, needing to look at the positive. "I entered the combine straight out of college. Luckily, I got picked up and I haven't looked back."

"What about your mom?" she asks, making me flinch. It doesn't matter that I knew the question was coming.

"She helped me heal and then she buried her head in the sand."

"Levi," she whimpers, her voice full of empathy.

Turning around to face her, I lean against the fence and hold her in my arms. Tears ripple down her cheeks. Reaching up, I gently wipe them away with my thumbs. "Please, don't cry for me, Layla. I'm one of the lucky ones. I got away."

My words only make her cry harder. Pulling her to my chest, I press my lips to the top of her head, inhaling her sweet scent. As she catches her breath, she rasps, "Thank you for telling me. I'm sorry to bring it up."

Sliding my fingers underneath her chin, I tip it up until she meets my gaze. "There's nothing to be sorry about. Now you know why I don't talk about it, but it also feels good to share it with someone. No one but my family knows the truth."

Taking a deep breath, she slides her hand up to my jaw, holding my gaze. "It means a lot to me for you to trust me with this." Pushing up on her tiptoes, she nudges my head towards hers and sweeps her lips across mine.

Not wanting her to get away, I lean into the kiss, our mouths sliding together, her lips soft and full. Tilting my head, my tongue flicks out, licking the seam of her mouth, her taste sweet like the wine she had earlier. She whimpers, her lips parting, just as she falls back on her heels, breaking our kiss. "Come home with me," I request, desperate to be near her. "We don't need to do anything, I just want you close."

"And is doing something off the table?" she asks, fluttering her lashes, her cheeks flushed.

Fuck me. I kiss her hard and tear my mouth away, linking our hands once again. I grin down at her, her eyes sparkling up at me with a tenderness that nearly crushes my heart. "Let's go."

Chapter 24

Layla

"A re you hungry?" Levi asks as we walk inside his place.

"Not really. Chloe and I had a bite to eat before book club."

He grins, turning towards me and gathering me into his arms. "I like your book club. Looks like I have a book to read this month. It sounds sinful."

My face heats, and I wrap my arms around his waist, burying my face in his chest. Inhaling deeply, I relish his clean, musky scent. "Don't say that again. It sounds weird coming out of your mouth."

He chuckles, pressing his lips to the top of my head. "Don't say what again? Sinful?"

"Yeah, that." His chest bounces lightly with his quiet laughter, bringing a smile to my face. "Besides, the best books have a good story and we've been reading so many with fantastic stories."

Thankfully, he remains silent and I melt further into him, savoring his warm embrace. Unfortunately, his earlier confession continues to slap me in the face. I thought my father was an asshole, but Levi's dad takes it to a whole different level and it breaks my heart. Guilt weighs on me for bringing it up, no matter how much he insists not to worry.

"You okay?" he prods, gently squeezing my side.

Lifting my head, I stare at him. "You shouldn't be the one asking me if I'm okay, Levi."

"It can go both ways."

"Are you okay?" I echo.

"Yes. I'm happy to be here with you." A lump forms in my throat and I give him a sad smile. Groaning, he pleads, "You have to stop with the looks, Layla. I'm fine. I promise. It was a long time ago."

"Sorry. I'm trying. Maybe I should take you up on that movie to redirect the mood."

"Or maybe we can make out like teenagers. That sure as hell will work with me." He smirks, his suggestion going straight to my core, heat pooling low in my belly.

"I like that idea," I reply, suddenly breathless.

Loosening his hold, he inches his hands up my sides. Weaving his fingers into my hair, he cradles my face in his hands. Staring into my eyes, his own melt into liquid gold. "You're so beautiful, Layla," he murmurs, reverent, causing my heart to leap. His lips brush mine in a whisper of a kiss. "Tell me if it's too much or too fast," he insists, his voice low and rough.

Not able to speak a response, I nod.

Agonizingly slow, he lowers his head towards mine, tilting it slightly before our lips touch in a tender kiss, igniting a bolt of electricity to travel throughout my body. A breathy sigh escapes and I pull him tighter. Our mouths move in tandem, unhurried, and sensual.

Breaking our kiss, his eyes roam my face, searching, his look intense and heated. His arms lower, slipping around my back. Holding my gaze, he stalks towards me, forcing me to walk backwards. The back of my feet hit something and he lowers me down onto the velvety couch cushions, leaning his body partially on the couch and the rest of him pressed up against me from head to toe, his hard length, firm against my stomach.

Levi's face falls into my neck and he inhales deeply, his tongue jutting out and licking a path up to my ear. He groans, sucking my lobe into his mouth, his teeth grazing my skin and then releasing it, eliciting an uncontrolled whimper.

"Levi," I pant, unsure what I'm asking.

Trailing his mouth along my jaw, his lips soon find mine and I tug him impossibly closer, kissing him hard, desperate. My lips part and his tongue slips inside, intertwining with mine. Licking, twisting, his sweet taste fills my senses. I moan into his mouth, wanting more.

Every inch of me prickles with awareness. My hands skim over his hard chest and up the ridges of his back. Sealing my mouth to his, I easily get lost in his kiss. Every move, and gentle touch, every lick, and tantalizing suck, everything about him and all he does sets me ablaze.

Breaking apart, we catch our breath, his forehead falling to mine. "The couch probably wasn't the best idea," pausing, he shifts, "just the closest." He chuckles, but he doesn't sound genuine.

My brows furrow. "What's wrong?" I ask, and I gasp the moment the words leave my mouth, my brown orbs widening as realization hits me. "Your arm. Oh, my gosh, Levi. Are you all right?" I stammer, gently nudging him up.

Wincing, he pushes up with his left hand and sits, rotating and stretching his right arm. "I'll be fine. I just moved wrong."

"I am so sorry. I'm the worst." Frantic, I sit up next to him, carefully checking his arm.

"The way you were just kissing me, Layla, you're the opposite of the worst. And I'm damn sure almost anything would be worth another kiss from you."

I huff a laugh. "Ever the charmer."

He smirks but doesn't comment. Extending his arm, he claims, "See? Already better."

My eyes narrow at him. "Maybe I should give you a massage and then we can ice it."

"I'm not going to argue with you anytime you want your hands on me, but I'm all right. I promise."

"Okay, but we have to be more careful next time."

"I'm always careful." A crooked smile covers his face.

I huff a laugh. "Good to know, but I'm serious."

"So am I," he says, bringing me back into his arms. "As long as there is a next time, I don't give a damn." He kisses me behind the ear.

"Levi," I rasp, savoring the feel of the smile on his lips as he presses another kiss to my neck. "No more."

"What?"

"I said no more. It's impossible to focus when you're doing that and I need to take care of you right now."

Sighing, he frowns and covers my mouth with a heated kiss, gliding over my lips in a perfect rhythm. He leans back all too quickly, and scowls. "Fine. As you wish. No more for now."

Laughing, I stand, and guide him to his room. "Lay on your side for me." He does as I say and I begin digging into his arm, massaging.

He moans. "You can do the rest of me if you want when you're done."

Giggling, I continue working on him, my hands drifting as he suggested when I'm done. He rolls onto his stomach when my heads wander onto his back, rubbing the hard ridges of his muscles, over his shoulder and along his spine. Drifting onto his ass, a smile curves my lips. Everything about his body is hard and smooth. I could do this all day.

Trailing my hands up and over his shoulders, I lean towards his face, admiring the softness of his features while relaxed.

"Levi?" I whisper.

Silence.

A light laugh slips out and I quickly cover my mouth to stifle it. He actually fell asleep. Gently, I press my lips to his temple and lean back, glancing down at him. "Goodnight, Levi."

Grabbing my things, I slip out the door before I get too comfortable, my thoughts focused on Levi. I'm done pretending. I can't fight it anymore. Our chemistry is obvious. He sparks my body to life with just a look. His kisses make me lose my mind. I want to be out of control with him. If he can kiss me like that, the things I believe he could do to my body have only been living in my fantasies, but I want them to be real.

For me, I know it's not just lust. I like Levi. He does unexpected things to my heart and I want to relish the feeling. Throwing away all my doubts and hesitation, I'm almost desperate to dive in headfirst and soak up every moment with him. My only hope is that he doesn't shatter my heart--shatter me.

But if I don't take the chance, the reward won't exist.

I'm ready to jump.

Chapter 25

Levi

Scrambling, I button my jeans and yank a black t-shirt on over my head. My nerves are haywire hoping everything falls into place. Grabbing my phone, I send a quick text to Layla.

A grin tugs at my lips when my phone vibrates almost instantly with her reply.

Chuckling, I type out a message.

> No. I'll see you in ten minutes. I just wanted you to know I've been thinking of you.

Layla

> I think the flowers you sent Tuesday, the chocolates yesterday and the wine you had delivered today do that well. Thank you again.

> You're welcome.

Layla

> And I can't wait to see you too.

A wide smile plasters across my face. I can't help it. She makes me feel like myself, not the player everyone knows and I fucking love it.

Before pocketing my phone, I send a quick text to Chloe.

> Just confirming you will all be there.

Chloe

> Yes, Levi. I've got you covered.

> Thank you.

I slip my phone in my pocket and grab the flowers and gift for Layla, along with my wallet and keys. Stepping outside, I glance up and see my aunt and uncle eating dinner at the table in the backyard.

"Hey, Levi," Uncle Steve says, nodding.

"Are you heading out now?" Aunt Miranda questions.

"Yes. I'm going to pick her up."

She smiles. "We'll be there soon. And Levi?" I arch my brow, waiting. "You're doing a nice thing for her. I'm really proud of the man you are."

"We're both proud of you," Uncle Steve emphasizes.

A lump forms in my throat. Coming from my aunt and uncle, their words, their conviction means so much more to me than it would be from my parents. Gulping, I rasp, "Thank you."

My aunt stands, giving me a hug, I return. Stepping back, she insists, "You deserve to be happy, Levi and like we said from the start, Layla is a sweet woman."

"Yeah, she's incredible."

"Let him go get his woman," Uncle Steve says, smirking at my aunt. "We'll see him soon."

Her cheeks turn pink. Chuckling, I wave and stride towards the front of the house.

Slipping into my car, I make the short drive to Layla's and park in her driveway. Climbing out, I grab the gifts, striding up the walkway. The front door swings open before I reach it, Gabe leaving.

"Going out?" Layla asks before noticing me. I take the moment to admire her beauty. Surprisingly, she's wearing her hair down, hanging loose over her shoulders. Dressed in a silky, rust colored top with spaghetti straps and an intricate design along the scoop neck and dark blue jeans with rhinestones on the back pockets she looks gorgeous. Her casually sexy look goes straight to my cock.

"I've got a hot date," he claims, smirking.

"Have fun," she says, just as her eyes land on me. "Hi."

Gabe waves to me as he passes, walking to his truck.

"Hi, Layla. You look beautiful."

Her cheeks darken, and a smile lights up her face. "Thanks. Do you want to come in?"

"Sure." I step closer, pausing in the doorway and handing her the fall bouquet and gift bag. "These are for you."

"You didn't have to do that. The other fall flowers and the sunflowers still look beautiful. I only have so many places to put flowers." She laughs, the light sound squeezing my heart as she closes the door behind me.

"No, I didn't have to, but I wanted to."

"Well, thank you." She sets the gift bag down, while she searches for another vase, filling it with water and placing the flowers, leaving them in the center of the small kitchen island.

"You're welcome. Why don't you open the present," I suggest wanting to see her open it.

"Okay." She walks over to the bag and rips out the tissue paper. "You've been spoiling me, Mr. Brennan."

I give her a salacious grin, my thoughts turning wicked. Licking my lips, I arch my brow, but she only laughs in response.

She takes out three romance books in a new series, provoking a shocked gasp. Her mouth drops open and snaps closed. Lifting her gaze, she holds mine. "How did you know I wanted these?"

Running my hand through my hair, I take a deep breath and admit, "I heard you talking to Chloe about them at book club last week."

Her eyes water, but the tears don't flow. Setting them down, she lunges for me, throwing her arms around me and holding me tight. "Thank you. This was so thoughtful, I can't even explain what this means to me."

"You're welcome. I'm glad you like them."

"Hopefully, I like the story as much as I like getting the gift from you." She laughs, releasing me and turning right back into me. Pushing up on her tiptoes, she presses her lips to mine, falling back almost immediately. "Just, thank you," she reiterates, squeezing me again.

"If this is what I get when I buy you a few books, I just may be buying you your own library."

She snorts, swiftly covering her mouth, but even her hand can't hide her pure glee. My heart hammers, ecstatic to witness her genuine reaction. "These were sold out everywhere. How did you get them?"

"I can't tell you all my secrets already." She giggles, shaking her head in disbelief and kisses me again, this time hard, unyielding, leaving me breathless.

My arms wrap around her back, her hands resting gently on my forearms. She falls back on her heels and I drop my head further, holding her close, my head pressing to her forehead. Clearing my throat, I rasp, "We should go before I cancel tonight and take you to your bedroom."

"Gabe will apparently be gone for a while."

My head falls back as I burst out laughing. If she only knew her statement did the opposite of enticing me to abandon our plans, she wouldn't be making the joke. "All right, you little vixen," I tease, nipping at her lower lip. "Let's go before we're late."

"Late for what?"

"I have reservations."

"But I already ate."

Chuckling, I reply, "I know. Let's go."

"Huh?"

Ignoring her confusion, I advise, "Grab your purse and sweater if you want them."

She does as I requested and rejoins me by the door. Reaching for her, I thread our fingers together and guide her out to my car. My smile remains glued to my face, treasuring my time with her and looking forward to the rest of the night.

"Where are we going?" she asks, nibbling on her lower lip.

Fighting the urge not to groan, I drive away from the curb, telling her, "It's a surprise."

"That's why you've been so secretive," she chimes, her lips curving up. "I like surprises. Will I like this one?"

Laughing, my heart fills, glancing at her out of the corner of my eye. "I sure hope so."

Chapter 26

Layla

I'm pretty sure I know where we're headed, but it's quickly confirmed when we turns into the same gravel parking lot where we picked out the pumpkins we still haven't carved. "Are we going on that haunted hayride?" I question, bouncing in my seat.

Levi parks his car and glances at me, grinning. "I did promise you we would come back for it."

"Yes! This will be so much fun!" I grin.

We step out of the car and he drapes his arm around my shoulders, drawing me close and pressing a kiss to the top of my head. "You told me you could handle scary things, but you never said if you actually like them. I hope this is okay," he prods, shifting slightly, suddenly appearing unsure.

Placing my palm on his chest, I look up at him, appreciating his concern. "I think they're fun, but I do get spooked too. I'm happy we're here." Pausing, I pat his chest for emphasis. "I promise." His shoulders relax, his anxiety draining out of him.

Strolling towards the back, we see a banner over a walkway, advertising *The Haunted Hayride*, but there's a rope across the path with a sign. "The Haunted Hayride is closed from 7:30-9 pm tonight for a private event," I read aloud, my disappointment clear. "No," I whine. "That sucks. I guess we'll have to come back."

"Or...Come with me," Levi urges, ducking under the rope and bringing me along with him.

"Levi, we're not supposed to be over here," I whisper, tugging on his hand. Anxiously, I look around as if someone is standing in the bushes waiting to catch trespassers and attack them.

Chuckling, he claims, "We are if we're the ones who reserved it."

It takes a moment for his words to register and when they do, I gasp, staring at him wide-eyed. "What did you do?"

He shrugs, a sexy crooked smile on his face and his eyes sparkling, fixing on me. "I didn't want to have fans infringing on our date like last time we were here. You should be my focus. Plus, I thought it would be a lot more fun to do this with our family and friends."

Before I comprehend his words, a voice sounding exactly like my brother calls out from off to the side. "They're finally here!"

Spinning towards the voice, I spot Gabe first, grinning broadly and my mom standing next to him. "Mom?" I question with apparent disbelief.

"Took you long enough," Gabe teases as we walk towards them, waiting near a small group of people.

"Hey, Layla." Chloe waves, holding Beck's hand with the other and her Nana, Nora, standing alongside them, grinning.

"Chloe!" I shriek in excitement. "What are you doing here?"

"Levi invited all of us," she answers, giving me a look that tells me she's happy for me.

"I wanted to surprise you," he says, unexpectedly bashful, running his free hand through his hair, keeping the other touching me at all times.

That's when I take a moment to look at the small group of people, seeing all the familiar faces. Levi's Aunt Miranda and Uncle Steve smile, watching from the back of the group. "Scotty?" I prompt, leaning against the hay wagon, with his arm protectively around his husband, George.

"Are you ready for this, Layla? I painted my fingernails to match the occasion," he says, wiggling his sparkly black, orange, and purple nails.

Tears blur my vision. "They look great, Scotty."

"Doesn't look like you can see anything," Gabe teases.

"Oh, hush," my mom chides him making him laugh.

Blinking back my tears, I look at Levi, my heart feeling like it's about to burst. If I had any doubt about my feelings for him before, he just made sure they were completely solidified. "Everyone I care about is here," I rasp, barely able to get the words out. He nods, his face flushing, still staring. "Do you have any idea what you've done?" I question, my voice cracking.

He opens his mouth to say something, but before he can speak, I grab the back of his head and pull him towards me, kissing him in front of everyone. Quickly, I fall back on my heels with a huge smile on my face, seeing Levi's cheeks turning red. "Thank you, Levi."

"I like seeing you happy, Layla. That's all that matters." My heart can't take another moment of this in front of everyone. As if reading my mind, he gestures behind me. "We should go."

Grinning, I glance at the man standing next to the four wooden steps leading up to the wagon. "Thank you," I say as I climb the steps. I walk across the wooden trailer and over to the bench seat up near the front where it's connected to a tow. A large black pickup truck is parked, waiting with its running lights on. My gaze finds Levi. "I'm glad that they don't use horses for this. I was worried they would get scared."

"You're probably right." He sits down next to me in the corner, his arm resting on the rail behind me. Chloe sits on my other side, with Beck in tow. "Don't you want to sit next to me, Chloe?" Nora probes, her tone playful.

Chloe shakes her head. "No, Nana. You'll make me jump before there's a reason to," she claims, Nora laughing in response as she sits next to Beck.

Levi's aunt and uncle take the seat across from Nora, with my mom next to them and Gabe on the other side, right beside Scotty and George, who are sitting directly across from us.

The man at the back, closes the gate and secures it, waving and backing away. "Good luck," he says, monotone, only some of us laughing.

"Ready?" a driver calls from the window of the pickup.

"All set," Levi answers, giving him a thumbs up.

Slowly, he starts moving and steers towards the cornfields, the path narrowing as we drive towards the darkness. Chloe huddles into Beck, the darker it gets, her face pressed into his shoulder. Scotty's eyes remain wide and cautious with George's focus on him. Gabe's eyes are filled with amusement as he leans back, relaxed as if ready for anything. Nora glances out of the corner of her eye at Chloe and suddenly stomps on the wood floor, Chloe screaming in response. "Nana!" she scolds, followed by Nora chortling.

Rustling leaves, snapping twigs and sounds of corn stalks cracking get closer. Scarecrows jump out from both sides, reaching through the wooden slats as if to grab us. I squeal, arching away and laughing, listening to Chloe and Scotty both screech.

As we go further, we enter into a constructed tunnel with bats flying overhead. Off to the side, a cemetery comes into view, the fog thick, and the air laced with the scent of dirt and decay. Zombies reach up through the muddied ground, clawing their way out of their graves and trudging towards us.

A tomb opens next to it, a mummy emerging. I lean into Levi, watching our friends and family, savoring this moment. "I can't believe you came for this," I whisper in Chloe's ear.

She glances at me, still clinging to Beck. "Yeah, you definitely owe me big time for this one. You and your boyfriend both."

Boyfriend. The word echoes in my mind. How the hell did that happen.

I look back at Levi and press a kiss to his lips. "Thank you," I reiterate, staring at him intently, trying to let him know how much this means to me.

A clawed hand comes down on the wooden slats between us and we both jump, me letting out a small scream. We laugh as I curl into him with a smile on my face and look back out into the darkness.

Strobe lights flicker and chains clatter in the distance as a science lab comes into view, the room splattered with blood on nearly every surface. A man dressed in a bloodied, torn lab coat and his goggles perched on the top of his head steps into the middle of the room cleaning blood from a hatchet. Dragging his gaze towards us, his mouth curls into an evil grin, trudging towards the vehicle making my heart pound.

As we make our way out of the cave, the moment we start to relax, chainsaws ignite, making me jump, and grasp frantically at Levi's waist. My palm splays on his chest, feeling his heart hammering just as hard as mine bringing a smile to my face. We both chuckle, as familiar horror movie icons step out of the corn from every direction, bloodied and yielding various weapons, stalking towards us.

Shrieks, screaming, and chaos ensues all around us.

It's absolutely perfect. Thanks to Levi.

Chapter 27

Layla

Slipping a red dress on over my head, adorned with white polka dots, I look in the mirror and frown at my reflection. The dress flares slightly at the waist, falling to just above my knees, but I'm not sure it's right for tonight. I want to look good for Levi, especially after what he did for me last night, but I rarely wear dresses. Playing with the spaghetti straps, I make sure my breasts are secure and tasteful, but wonder if it's too much.

Grabbing my phone off my dresser, I snap a picture and send it to Chloe with a short text.

Yay or nay?

Chloe

Absolutely yay! For Levi?

Yes. Who else would it be for?

I do as she suggested, brushing my hair up and wrapping the ponytail with a red ribbon. Pairing my outfit with my cherry red heels, I slip them on, hooking the strap around my ankle and take one more look in the mirror, trusting my best friend. I send her one more picture for affirmation.

I stick my ID and my debit on the back of my phone just in case and slip both in the pocket of my dress. Stepping out of my room, I run into Gabe, his eyes widening in surprise. "Where are you headed?"

"A date with Levi."

He smirks. "Have fun. I'm going out with a couple friends later, so I won't be here either."

"Okay," I mumble, dragging out the word, waiting like he has more he's about to say, but holds back. A knock sounds at the door, interrupting us. Grinning, I spin on my heel, striding towards the door, and wave to him over my shoulder. "I'll see you later, Gabe."

I open the door and find Levi standing there dressed in dark blue jeans and a black button down with the sleeves rolled up to his elbows and the top two buttons open making my mouth water. Licking his lips, he grips another bouquet of flowers in his hand, with his eyes as wide as saucers and his mouth gaping.

"Shit," he mumbles under his breath. His Adam's apple bobs up and down as he gulps hard, blinking as if he's not sure what he's seeing is real. "What the fuck are you trying to do to me?" he rasps, his words a low growl.

My brows furrow. "You don't like it?"

He huffs a laugh and steps towards me. "You're kidding right?" He closes the distance between us and wraps the hand with the flowers around my waist dragging me into him, his hard shaft pressing into my stomach. Gasping, my eyes flare, heat pooling low in my belly. "I absolutely love it. You are not only gorgeous, Layla, but you're so damn sexy."

My cheeks flush, and my heart lurches, a smile curving my lips. "Thank you, Levi."

Tipping his head down, he sucks my bottom lip between his and then kisses me, soft and slow, eliciting a content sigh.

Gabe clears his throat from somewhere behind me, breaking us apart. Levi lifts his head, reluctantly releasing me and I turn to face my brother. "I thought you were going out?" he taunts, chuckling.

We're leaving, now," I claim. Taking the flowers from Levi, I ask, "Are these for me?"

"Of course."

Turning back to my brother, I hold out the flowers. "Here. Since you're staying with me, rent free, you can put these in some water for me and we'll get out of your hair."

"Thanks," Levi smirks, nodding towards Gabe.

Heaving a sigh, he takes the flowers from me. "Fine. Have fun, you two, but not too much."

"Bye, Gabe," I say, threading my fingers through Levi's and tugging him out my front door.

"You have everything?"

"Yup," I respond, popping the p, feeling playful.

I slip into the passenger seat and he closes the door behind me, running his hand through his hair as he strides around the front of the car. The moment he gets behind the wheel, he shakes his head, chuckling low. "This is going to be a long night." He reaches over tangling our fingers and flipping his hand so mine covers his, resting on the gear shift.

"I really can't explain what last night meant to me, Levi."

He glances at me out of the corner of my eye before his eyes drift back to the road. "I'm glad you had fun." Clearing his throat, he informs me, "So, the plan is still to hit the new horror movie before dinner?"

"Yes, sounds good."

He nods and turns the music up for the short drive to the theater. A few minutes later, the scent of buttered popcorn hits my senses as we walk through the doors. "Mmm, that smells so good." I hum, Levi stepping right in line.

With popcorn, chocolate and drinks in hand, we make our way into the darkened theater, filled with red velvet seats and matching curtains framing the big screen at the front of the room. On each side of the screen, at the second level, a rounded box sits, overlooking the theater. They usually remain empty here and are only used for special guests or specific occasions, but Levi leads me directly to the one on the right. Unhooking the rope, he holds his arm out for me, gesturing for me to go first.

Quirking my brow, I ask, "Let me guess, you rented this too?"

He chuckles. "No, but I'm hoping the tip I just gave the usher will keep him from kicking us out."

I giggle, sitting down in one of the sparse seats, half the floor barren. "You're something else, Levi Brennan."

Sitting down next to me, he probes, "You just full-named me. Hopefully that's a good thing."

"With you it seems to be." Grinning, I press my lips to his, and move away as the movie starts.

Levi's hand falls to my knee, lightly tracing patterns on my bare skin. Within five minutes, someone is already dead and I don't remember how it happened, my focus solely on the gentle touch of Levi's fingers, slowly inching up my hemline.

Tingles spread across my skin like wildfire. "Levi," I say his name in warning.

Leaning in, I feel his heated breath on my neck, eliciting goosebumps. "I'll stop if you want me to, but there are so many things I want to do to you in this dress and I'm fighting to keep my hands to myself. It's killing me to wait almost a second more to touch you." I gasp, my entire body suddenly burning with desire. My breathing picks up its pace, but I'm afraid to move and break the moment. "No one can see you, the wall blocks you from your shoulders down."

"Are you sure?"

"I wouldn't take a chance with you," he claims, staring into my eyes.

"Okay."

With my whispered response, he brings my hand to his mouth and kisses my palm. Dropping it back to my lap, he slides his hand away from mine and drags his hand back to my knee. Slipping underneath the hem of my dress. He trails his fingers up the inside of my thigh, my breath catching in my throat. "Press your face into my chest or my neck when it's too much, and if you need me to stop, tell me," he instructs. Nibbling my lower lip in anticipation, I nod in response.

"I need to hear your answer."

"Okay."

"Good girl."

His whispered words of recognition send a thrill of excitement through my body, followed swiftly by his tender touch making me jump. Grasping my thigh, he holds me in place, my breath releasing along with his grip. Inching his fingers upwards, he skims the seam of my panties. Sliding them underneath the elastic, he releases a harsh exhale the moment he comes into contact with my wet folds. "You're soaked," he rasps, his own body stiffening.

Sucking my lower lip between my teeth, I bite down, holding back the sounds suddenly desperate to escape.

Readjusting, his knuckles run over my seam before he slips one finger inside me. Gliding it back to my clit, he circles it, once, twice, and repeats the move with two fingers, curling them inside me, pulling back and sliding it around three times. He pinches my clit, rolling it between his fingers, my insides burning.

I squirm, squeezing my eyes shut and burying my face in his chest, but it only gives him better access. His fingers work harder and faster, adding pressure with his thumb. My core burns and my insides swell, every touch, every move igniting me. Tremors of electricity shoot through me like I'm on a live wire, desperate to be extinguished, and eager for relief.

"It's okay, Layla," he whispers just above my hear, his breath hot and heavy, as if giving me permission. "Let go for me."

Screams ricochet around the theater, jolting me and pushing me to the edge ready to jump. His thumb presses firmly against my clit, and I fall, shattering around him. His fingers work their way in and out of my pussy as my walls squeeze him over and over again. With a harsh exhale, my body sags against him, spent.

He kisses the top of my head and carefully eases his hand out from under my skirt. Lifting my head, I glance at him, his heated gaze running over me. I lean on his shoulder, watching when he bends his arm, lifting his hand to his lips. Inhaling deeply, he traces his lips with my juices, his tongue jutting out and licking them clean. "Mm. Damn, I can't wait to really taste you."

The softest whimper escapes. I want that. I'm so ready for more with him. "Can we order in?" I ask, breathless. A chuckle of agreement falls from his lips, a salacious grin in place.

Chapter 28

Levi

"Mm. Those tacos were absolutely delicious. Thank you," Layla says, licking her lips, making me want to take a bite of her.

Clearing my throat, I stand, saying, "You're welcome." Leaning down, I give her a chaste kiss, but it's not nearly enough. Grabbing our plates, I carry them into the kitchen to clean up, not able to sit still.

Layla follows me, leaning her elbows against the counter and pushing up her cleavage. Fuck. "Want some help?" she asks.

"No, thanks. I got it." I focus on rinsing the dishes and placing them in the dishwasher. At the moment that's all I can handle. Layla my sole focus.

My hands are itching to touch her again, but this time, I want to be able to spread her out on my bed and explore every part of her. Watching her fall apart knowing no one could see what I was doing to her was priceless. I wanted to bend her over, flip up her dress and fuck her right there, but getting arrested, or having her exposed to anyone else is not high on my priority list. Although seeing her completely uninhibited with me just might be at the top of it.

We walk back into the living room and she shifts near the couch, as if she's unsure what she wants to do. I stalk towards her, holding her gaze. "You know, you're always gorgeous, Layla. You have this elegant beauty like no other woman I've ever met, but there's something about you in this dress that is absolutely driving me wild," I proclaim, watching her beautiful brown orbs enlarge, her full lips loosely pucker and her face heat.

Stepping towards her, I reach up, cradling her face in my hands. Tipping my head down, I brush my lips over hers, savoring the feel of having her near, her warm breath on my face, our hearts pounding in anticipation. Finally, eliminating the distance between us, I kiss her, keeping my movements tender, measured, attempting to show her how much I care. Closing my eyes, I tilt my head and deepen our kiss, feeling her body melting into mine. My insides blaze, and I struggle to hold back, my dick fighting me. But I refuse to push too hard or move too fast. Not with Layla.

Planting her palms on my chest, she gently nudges me back, breaking our kiss. Leaning my head on her forehead, we stand, unmoving, both of us catching our breath. She glances at me, licking her lips as if she wants to say something.

"Layla? Are you all right?"

"I just have to ask you something."

"Okay," I say, drawing out the word.

"You're not with anyone else, are you?" she blurts out, hesitant, but determined.

Frowning, I straighten, my stomach suddenly churning. Holding her gaze, I insist, "Hell no. Layla, I don't want anyone but you. Please tell me you're not seeing, dating, or especially not sleeping with anyone else. Now that I've found you, I'm not about to share with anyone."

Giggling, she pats my chest. "Slow down, Levi. You are the only man in my life I want to date or sleep with."

I breathe a sigh of relief, a cheeky grin tugging at the corners of my mouth. "Good. Let's keep it that way."

Smiling, she leans into me once again. "I'd like that."

Staring into her eyes, I need her to know the truth in my words. "I'm serious, Layla. I'm not the man you met at the diner."

"That's a damn good thing." She smirks.

Chuckling, I kiss her again.

Nudging me back, she requests, "Do you mind if we move this to your room. I don't want you hurting your arm again."

My chest tightens at the same time as my cock and I grin. "You are always welcome in my bed." Spinning her around, my hands rest on her shoulders and I guide her to my room. "This way."

She steps through the door and away from me, sitting on a small bench near the footboard. "Sorry, I need to take these shoes off. I haven't worn them in a long time."

"Let me help." Getting down on one knee, my palm curves around the smooth skin of her calf, unhooking the strap before slipping it off and setting it on the floor. Grabbing her other leg, I do the same and she rises, standing before me. I look up at her and am momentarily overwhelmed.

Shaking myself out of my stupor, I take a deep breath and slowly rise. Skimming my hands up her legs, her skirt bunches up slightly before it falls. Her breathing picks up its pace as my hands settle at the top of her ass.

"Levi," she whispers.

Leaning down, no longer able to hold back, I seal my mouth over hers, kissing her hard. My tongue juts out, begging for entrance and she eagerly opens, her tongue immediately tangling with mine. Slowly guiding her around the corner of the bed, I continue licking, tasting and exploring her mouth, our tongues playfully fighting for dominance.

When I have her against the side of the bed, my hand wraps around the silky strands of her ponytail, gently urging her head backwards as I kiss a path down her neck and over her collarbone.

My hand skims her side, palming her breast, feeling her already pert nipple arch into me.

"Fuck," I mutter, gently squeezing, my thumb running over her nipple and pinching over the fabric of her dress.

"I want this off, Levi."

"Not yet. Lay back on the bed," I instruct. She does as I ask, keeping her gaze fixed on me bringing a smile to my face. "Good girl."

My words have her body heating and I fucking love it. I kiss her again, my hands trailing her sides and slipping underneath her dress. Hooking my fingers in the sides of her panties, I slide them down her legs, dropping them to the floor. Gliding my hands back up her legs, I push her skirt up to her waist, exposing her sweet pussy with a narrow strip of dark hair down to her sweet spot. "Damn, you're gorgeous."

"Levi," she rasps, already breathless.

My hands grip her thighs, gently parting her legs as I kneel between them. Leaning towards her, I inhale deeply, cherishing her intoxicatingly sweet scent. "Mm..." My tongue juts out, licking her folds. I hum, savoring her taste. "Fuck, you taste good." I lick her again, sucking her clit into my mouth and flicking my tongue around it. Moving back, I push my tongue inside her pussy, curling and pushing firm along her folds, circling and sucking her clit again. I repeat the motion, tasting her juices, feeling her heat and swell towards me.

"Levi," she whimpers. Curling, circling and sucking, I flatten my tongue, pressing firm and repeating the motions. Her hands tangle into my hair, tugging and holding me to her at the same time. Her breathing becomes rapid, and she gasps for breath, repeating my name again and again. Every sound, every touch spurs me on and then she falls--pulsing, moaning, clenching, begging, and soaking my tongue until she stops moving completely, focusing on just breathing. "Oh, my god, Levi. That was..."

I smirk, crawling up her body, pressing kisses to any exposed skin along the way. Brushing my lips over hers, I settle into her side, my dick digging into her hip, begging to be released, but I don't want to assume anything. "You okay?"

"I'm fantastic." She glances at me and frowns. "But you have too many clothes on and you're not supposed to be in that position."

"Sorry. It's a bad habit."

"Yes, it is. Take your shirt and pants off and lay down."

I arch my brow. "Yes, ma'am."

She giggles and leans up on her elbows, watching as I reach back with one hand and yank my shirt over my head, dropping it on the floor. Holding her gaze, I unbutton my jeans and kick them off, along with my boxer-briefs. Her eyes widen and she stares at my hard, erect cock as I climb on the bed and lay back, waiting to see what she'll do.

Licking her lips, she asks, "Dress on or off?"

I open my mouth to answer but surprise myself when I hesitate. "What are we doing? Your answer could make all the difference."

"It's my turn to taste you."

My heart pounds against my ribcage. Those words coming out of her mouth as she looks at my cock like she's ready to devour it almost makes me come before she even comes close to me. I groan. "Damn, Layla. Let's start with the dress on and if I accidentally rip it, I'll buy you another just like it."

She straddles me, kissing me, but quickly backs away, licking and kissing her way down my chest, every touch going straight to my dick. Her full breasts are nearly spilling out of her dress, and her panties are on my floor.

Shit. I'm not going to last. Embarrassingly so. There's no fucking way. I'm about to lose it. Her hands graze my cock, followed by the warm, rough feel of her tongue. She swirls it around the tip before she wraps her perfect full lips around my cock giving me the perfect image to cum to for the rest of my damn life. Sucking me into her mouth, she takes me to the back of her throat, licking and sucking. She moves faster, sucking me hard and firm. Heat shoots low in my gut and I grab her ponytail and lightly yank her back.

"Layla, babe, that feels so good, but I don't want to come like this. I want to be inside you if you'll let me."

She falls back and crawls over me, straddling me. "Condom?" she asks.

Reaching up, I cup her jaw, staring into her eyes. "I want you, Layla, but are you sure this is what *you* want?"

"Yes, I want you, Levi."

My heart lurches as if she just declared her love. "In the drawer," I say, pointing to the nightstand.

Reaching over, she grabs what she needs. I hold my hand out, but she shakes her head. "Let me do it." My dick jumps, straining towards her as she rips the wrapper and grasps the condom, rolling it on. Looking down at me, she informs me, "I'm staying on top."

Goosebumps prickle my skin at her command, loving that she's taking charge. "Yes, ma'am." I smirk, my hand trailing down her center to her core. Watching her reactions, I graze her slippery folds and pinch her clit, rolling it between my thumb and forefinger and slide back, inserting one finger and then two, a sexy moan falling from her lips. Removing them, I glide them over her pussy, applying pressure.

Planting her hands on my chest, she pushes away from me, raising herself up and hovering over my rigid cock. My hands go to her hips, gripping her. With one hand she shimmies her skirt out of the way, keeping the other on my chest and torturously slow, lowers herself down on me, every inch pure ecstasy. "Oh, wow," she pants.

Her tight walls squeeze me and I grip her hips, controlling my breathing. "Shit, you're tight."

"It's been a while," she murmurs, that fact hitting me hard. "I feel so full."

Slowly, she moves up and down, before circling her hips and then doing it again. Everything about her and this moment, this feeling, erotic. My fingers dig into her thighs, clinging to my control, but seeing her ride me in this fucking dress...I'll never be the same.

My heartbeat quickens, breathing intensifies, and my body combusts with my hips bucking up to meet her. Knowing this time I won't last, I reach down, my thumb finding her clit, and flicking, rubbing it in circles and applying pressure desperate to feel her release surround me. "Layla, I need you to come for me, please," I beg.

Her tits bounce every time she slides up and down my hard shaft making me impossibly harder. Hooded eyes meet mine, her chest heaving as she rides me faster, seeking her orgasm and bringing me to the brink along with her.

"I'm..." she rasps, trailing off.

Continuing to move with her in a rhythm that's all our own, she whimpers as her hot, wet pussy squeezes my cock. She tremors, clenching and unclenching. A guttural groan leaves my lips as I completely lose control. Thrusting upwards, her walls squeeze me, milking me stimulating a heat exploding low in my belly. Her juices coat my dick as she starts to come down from her high, my own movements becoming erratic as I come, shooting my load into the condom.

She collapses on top of me, just as I finish, both of us sweaty and gasping for breath. My hand falls to her back and I pull her closer to my lips. Kissing her, I request, "Stay with me?"

Her eyes widen in surprise. I get it. If it were any other woman I wouldn't be asking, but I no longer want anyone else. "Okay. Got a shirt for me to wear?"

Chuckling, I ask, "Does that mean I finally get to see what's really under that dress?"

"No. You made your choice, now you have to live with it," she says, but it's hard to believe she means it with that smile on her face.

Approaching the dresser, I find a pair of clean boxer shorts for me to sleep in and a black t-shirt for her. Walking back to the bed, I hold my hand out for her and she comes willingly. "On your knees," I say, my eyes glinting with mischief.

"You're trouble, Mr. Brennan."

"Well, that can make things a whole lot of fun."

Chapter 29

Layla

My eyes flutter open, my cheek pressed to a warm, hard chest, Levi's heart beating against me. A small smile curves my lips as I cuddle closer to him. Last night was so much more than I imagined. My body tingles, thinking of the way Levi looked at me, the way he touched me, kissed me, and cherished me.

Chloe was right. There are men who really do know what they're doing in all aspects of the bedroom and Levi Brennan is one of them. A rare breed.

"Good morning," he rasps sending goosebumps down my spine.

Lifting my head, I meet his sleepy gaze, his hair sticking up in every direction looking sexy and bringing a smile to my face. "Good morning. I didn't realize you were awake."

"Only for a few minutes. Did you sleep okay?" he asks, running his fingers through my now loose hair.

"Yes."

"Are you hungry? We could make breakfast." His eyes shine down at me, his voice light, hopeful.

"I'm sorry, Levi, but I think I have to say no. I promised my brother we would go over some things for my mom today and then I need to go check on her."

His face falls and he nods. "Okay. I expect it's not something you would want company for?"

"Unfortunately, I don't think that's a good idea."

Tipping his head towards me, he hesitates before asking, "We're good?"

Giving him a broad smile, I give him a chaste kiss and sigh happily, speaking over his lips, "Yeah."

Exhaling slow, his body relaxes beneath me. Pulling me closer, he deepens our kiss, his tongue sweeping inside much too quick. "Good. I like waking up with you in my arms."

He kisses me again, sweet and slow, our tongues tangling and igniting me once again, but I force myself to nudge him back. "You can't get me going right now. I really do have to go. Besides, I'm a little sore."

He frowns, his hands skimming my sides. "Then come back later and I'll take care of you. After all, it's my fault you're sore." His lips find my neck, kissing, licking, gently sucking.

I hum, giggling. "Levi, you're relentless."

"Apparently, I am when it comes to you."

Kissing him again, I concede, "Okay, if I get everything done, I'll come back later. Does that work for you?"

"Absolutely. And while you're gone, I'll get my workout and exercises done, so I'll be free for you. My physical therapist is very demanding." He gives me his sexy smirk making my stomach twist.

"Remember to stick only with the exercises I gave you," I instruct, trying to keep my focus on the work instead of him. He's too distracting.

He chuckles and kisses me again. "Yes, ma'am."

A little while later, I walk in my front door wearing the same thing I left in last night. Slipping off my heels, I heave a sigh as my bare feet touch the cool wood floor. Lifting my head, I spot Gabe sitting on the couch eating a bowl of cereal watching sports center. He glances up at me and smirks. "Just getting home, Layla? Did you have a fun night?"

This is new. I never did a walk of shame growing up. Then again, I'm too old to be embarrassed about it now. Pasting a smile on my face, I drop down on the opposite end of the couch. "I did. How about you?"

His face falls but he drops the subject taking another bite of his cereal. "I have some places for us to go over virtually that I think have potential."

My throat clogs, not ready to have this conversation, but apparently we don't have a choice. Clearing my throat, I tell him, "Okay, sounds good, but I'm going to go shower first."

He scrunches up his nose. "Good! I was gonna say something..."

"Ha. Ha," I mutter, monotone.

"Oh, and by the way, I have a travel baseball camp thing I volunteered for this week a couple towns over. They have a fall break, so there's no school. It's long hours, so they're housing us. I can't back out now."

"It's all right, Gabe."

"You sure? I won't be around until the weekend."

"Like you said, you can't back out now, so what else could you possibly do?"

He sighs, shrugging. "I don't know, but this is why we have to find something. Once I'm back to baseball my schedule is rigid."

"I know. It's fine."

He shakes his head. "No, it's not, but any chance you can check on mom more this week?"

"Of course, I can. Maybe I'll even be able to get some help too."

"You think Levi would help?"

"Maybe," I admit, but is that too much to ask someone you just started dating? It feels like it is. "But I was thinking I could ask Chloe too. I'm sure she would help."

"Oh, yeah. Her boyfriend is a nice guy. I had fun talking to him the other night at the hayride."

"Yeah, I'm really happy for her. I like Beck and I like having her here."

"And what if we end up moving?"

My frown deepens. "I'm not sure, but I do know Chloe will always be in my life no matter where I am. She's stuck with me forever."

As for Levi, the possibility of moving is one of the biggest reasons I don't want to ask him for help with my mom. We're barely into a relationship yet we both might be moving to separate states soon. Is it fair to depend on each other when we can only offer right now? My own question slams into me like a tsunami inciting more doubt.

Is that what we are—temporary?

Heaving a sigh, I shove down the chaos attempting to take root in my head before it takes over. I just need to take things one day at a time with my mom, with Levi and with my future.

I can't stop the niggling voice in my head and my heart telling me that I want Levi to be a part of both my present and my future. Maybe that voice is not as insignificant as I'm pretending.

What if it's right?

Chapter 30

Layla

Stepping through Levi's back gate, I gasp at the beauty. Walking through their yard, tonight, looks like a pixie garden with fairy lights draped around the fence, sweeping along the roofline and hanging across the bar. The pool lights are glittering, looking like a tropical haven with the waterfalls flowing. White, electric candles flicker inside beautiful, black, wrought iron lanterns placed on every table throughout the space.

"Wow, it's beautiful," I murmur to myself, momentarily in awe.

Levi's voice brings my attention back to them. "Hi. Sorry, to interrupt," I say, cautiously approaching Levi standing with his Uncle Steve.

They turn towards me. "Hi, Layla," Steve greets me.

Levi grins. "Hi, you came back."

"I did. Gabe and I got everything done, for now anyway and I just left my mom's."

"Did you get a chance to eat? We've got a lot of leftovers," Steve offers. "With the kids home, I think Miranda cooked for an entire baseball team."

Giving him an appreciative smile, I decline. "Thank you, but I just had dinner with my mom."

"Then, I think I'll be heading inside. Thanks for helping out, Levi," his uncle says, making a quick exit.

"No problem," he acknowledges.

Facing me, he gathers me into his arms and tips his head down, pressing his lips against mine. "Hi, beautiful."

My heart soars at his compliment. "Hi. Sounds like you had a fun day today with your family."

Chuckling, he says, "If you want to call it that."

"Your cousins are home?"

"Yeah, they have a family wedding this week on Aunt Miranda's side, so they took a few extra days off. I didn't know about it until today."

"I get it. What are you helping out with?"

"Today, a lot of cleaning, and stuff around the yard since they'll be having other family in and out."

"That was nice of you, but did you overdo it? You didn't hurt yourself again did you?"

He chuckles, shaking his head. "No. I promise, I only did things I know I can do without you kicking my ass, but after everything they do for me, there was no way I was going to just sit and watch. But I am exhausted."

"I can go if you want."

"Please stay. I was thinking that a bath might be good for both of us," he suggests, wiggling his brows playfully. A salacious grin tugs at his lips as he watches me. My breath catches, and my skin prickles with awareness.

Without answering, I follow him inside and let him guide me towards the bathroom, suffused in an elegant silver and white. My gaze veers to him, watching as he turns the faucet of a large white clawfoot tub placed beside a silver and white shower adorned with a frosted glass door. Dipping his hand underneath the stream, he checks the water.

Stepping away, he looks at me and closes the distance between us. He slides his hands up my arms and cups the back of my neck, with his thumbs tenderly caressing the back of my jaw near my ears. Staring into my eyes with an intensity that causes my heart to stutter and my breath to hitch, he rasps, "I'm really happy you came back."

"Me too," I whisper.

His golden orbs glimmer, taking me in with a vulnerability that leaves me feeling open and splayed just for him.

"Layla, I meant it when I said I wanted to take care of you tonight. I know you're sore and we're both tired, but I just want to be with you and spend time with you. Let's take a bath, and then we can cuddle, talk, or just go to sleep. Together."

"That sounds perfect."

With my agreement, he grabs lavender and salts, adding the perfect amount. His actions, prompt me to ask, "Do you take a lot of baths, Levi?"

He chuckles. "Never with a beautiful woman." A snort escapes before I can stop it and I quickly cover my mouth, my cheeks turning red. Pressing his lips together, he shakes his head. "I'm serious. With sore muscles, you figure out ways to relax pretty damn fast. But it's always just me, except for the days I get put in one at our facility and my teammates definitely look nothing like you."

Disappointment in myself slices through me. I should know better than to assume the worst and judge him for it without asking him for the truth. Men take baths too. It doesn't have to be with another woman. "I'm sorry."

"I get it, but I'm already looking forward to the day you trust me."

"Levi–" I open my mouth to argue.

Pressing his lips to mine, he stops me from talking. Breaking our kiss, he tips his head back, assessing my reaction. "It will happen," he declares with immense confidence. "We just need time together."

Surprising myself, I believe him.

He rips off his shirt and tosses it on the floor. My lips part, mouth-watering at the sight of his hard abs. His shorts go next, but he momentarily leaves his boxers, giving me a view I can't tear my gaze from. Stepping up to me, he grips the hem of my shirt, arching his brow, waiting for my permission. I nod and he lifts it over my head, dropping it next to his.

My breathing picks up its pace. "I've got it," I tell him, forcing certainty.

Levi moves back, giving me some space. I step out of my skirt first, standing in front of him in just my bra and panties my heart an erratic mess beneath my ribcage. Reaching back, I unhook my bra and let it fall to the floor. His eyes widen, turning to liquid gold. Gripping my panties, I slide them down my legs and step out of them, straightening. Standing in front of him bare, exposed, his eyes flare, raking over my body and boosting my confidence. "You're even more beautiful than I imagined."

I blush, prickles racing through my insides. "Levi," his name falls from my lips on a soft sigh.

Turning off the water, he drops his boxers and steps into the tub, holding out his hand for me to follow. Carefully lowering himself in the tub, he leans back, opening his legs for me. I step in and sit down, submersing myself in the bubbles and facing away. The scent of lavender floods my senses, further relaxing me. His gentle touch on my back with the cottony soft washcloth starts to calm my racing heartbeat.

"Is this, okay?" he prompts.

"Yes," I answer breathlessly.

"Lean back," he directs. I do as he says, his hands gliding over my shoulders. Taking the washcloth, he runs it down my neck and arms. Painstakingly making his way along my sides and over my belly before reaching my breasts, pausing to take extra care, my nipples perking in delight. "You're perfect, Layla."

"Your flattery is doing wonders to my confidence."

"It's the truth. I'm wondering how I got so lucky to be here with you," he says, kissing my shoulder.

"Levi," I whisper, my heart squeezing. This is the time to tell him, talk to him.

He drags the cloth down to my legs, tenderly cleaning between them causing a shock of heat to burn through me. His breath becomes ragged, his cock pressing into my back. He chuckles darkly. "This is definitely a lesson in restraint."

Grabbing his hand, I ask, "Do you want me to wash you?"

He shakes his head. "That is definitely a very bad idea. Why don't you just lean back against me?"

Relaxing against his shoulder, I look up at him and smile. His arms wrap around my waist and I rest my hands on his solid forearm. "If you couldn't play baseball anymore, what do you think you would do?" I ask, instead of confessing.

"Is there something you're not telling me?"

"No, no, no! Nothing like that," I insist. "I'm sorry. You're healing well. I can tell you're listening to my advice even when I'm not around."

I feel his sigh of relief. "Well, I enjoy working at the camps with the high school kids and I would love to coach, but I think I'd like to be a pitching coach more than anything at the older levels. Pro, college, even high school. But if not in baseball," he pauses in thought, "maybe an announcer or sports broadcasting?" He chuckles. "I guess that's baseball too."

"It's okay. You obviously have a passion and you should follow it."

"What about you? Would you consider doing physical therapy for a pro team?" he asks, making my stomach turn as he gives me even more of a perfect opening.

"Um, well, I..." I stammer, trying to figure out how to tell him.

"I'm not saying you want any special treatment. That's not what I'm asking," he quickly amends, guilt hitting me for not speaking up.

"I don't know. Maybe, I..." I trail off, my heart hammering and my hands trembling with nerves.

"You're shaking. Let's get out. The water is getting cold."

Scrambling out of the tub, he grabs a towel and holds it up for me. I climb out and he quickly wraps me in the luxurious warmth, pressing a kiss to my temple. He reaches over and drains the water before grabbing his own towel and swiftly drying off, then, hanging it up. My gaze drops to his sculpted ass when we step into the bedroom, flicking back to his face as he grabs out a gray t-shirt, handing it to me. I drag it over my head before dropping the towel, seeing him stepping into a pair of boxers.

"You know we never carved our pumpkins."

He chuckles. "No, we didn't. We could always do it after you finish work tomorrow."

"Okay."

"Come on," he urges, linking our fingers and gently tugging me towards the bed. He tosses the covers back and gets in bed, beckoning me to him. I lay down facing him with one hand under my head. Smirking, he reaches for me and grips my hips, pulling me closer, a soft squeal escaping. "Closer."

Giggling, I say his name, "Levi."

"I just want to hold you and look at you," he murmurs. His hand grazes over my hair, stopping at the rubber band and jerking it loose. "You're so beautiful."

"And you're so sweet to me, Levi." I'm starting to wonder if I deserve it, if he deserves more than me.

"I want to do more for you if you'll let me." Closing the distance between us, he seals his mouth over mine, his kiss tender. Falling back to the pillow, his eyes flutter closed and I curl into his embrace, savoring our time together.

Chapter 31

Levi

After Halloween, I fall into my regular pattern of working out, physical therapy and a few easy baseball drills Layla will allow me to do, but now I have the added benefit of spending time with Layla, which is anything but routine. I have to admit, my time with her, even if it's for my physical therapy has become my favorite parts of my day.

I glance at the time, a smile creeping up on my face knowing she'll be done with work at the high school soon. Heading towards the shower to get cleaned up, I consider our plans for tonight.

My cell phone rings, garnering my attention. I swipe it off the table, looking at the screen. Joey, the manager for the Lions, lights it up causing my stomach to turn. He never calls for anything good during the offseason. Frowning, I clear my throat and swipe to answer. "Hey, Joey. How are you?"

"Hi, Levi. Sorry to bother you during your time off."

"No worries. What's up?"

"Just checking in for an update. How's the arm?" And there it is. His reason. Will I be able to perform next season? Is it worth it with my salary? Am I worth it?

"It's doing pretty good. In fact, I just got finished doing some drills. My physical therapist has been working me hard."

"All right, okay. Sounds good. I should be getting her update this week as well, but I wanted to hear things directly from you. Of course there's time, but it's good to see you're making progress." I flinch, his comment feeling like a death sentence. "Thanks, Brennan."

"Yeah, no problem."

He disconnects before saying anything else and my stomach plummets. I didn't like the feel of that call. What the fuck did that mean? Are they looking to trade me? Bench me? Send me down? What?

My anxiety increases wading into the unknown. I hate the politics of the game. I just wanna play.

Knowing I won't be able to sit still after that, I text Layla.

> Hey. Hope you had a good day. Sorry to cancel at the last minute, but I need to head to the indoor training facility over in Balan.

Layla

> It's okay. Everything all right?

> Yes. I'll text you when I'm on my way back if it's not too late.

Layla

> Okay. Take it easy on your arm.

Yes, ma'am.

Redirecting, I grab my gear, wallet and keys, heading for the door. On edge, I send one more text to Salinger, one of my teammates.

Hey Sal. Hope your enjoying vacation. Curious. Have you heard any trade rumors?

I press send and jump in the car. The moment I drive away, my phone rings, my Bluetooth alerting me to the call through my speakers. "Felix Salinger calling. Would you like to answer it?"

"Yes," I respond and immediately it connects me. "Sal, hey. How are you, man?"

"You don't call, you don't write, I'm hurt, Brennan," he jokes. "But I'm good besides. I saw your text and had to call. How's the arm?"

"Fuck the arm. It's fine. It's good. It's great."

He chuckles. "You sure about that."

Heaving a sigh, I laugh at myself. "Yeah, but I'm still sick of that damn question and after hearing from Joey–"

"You heard from Joey?" he interrupts. "What the fuck did he want?"

"I don't exactly know besides wanting to know how my arm is healing," I concede.

"Doesn't he get your PT reports?"

"Of course he does."

"Wait, is that why you're calling?"

"You called me," I remind him.

"Yeah, yeah. You know what I mean."

"I guess I wanted to know if you've heard any rumors going around about trades. You're always the first one to know. Usually even before the player."

"That's what happens when you're dating the boss's daughter. It has its perks," he teases, the smile in his voice apparent.

"How are things with Angelica?"

"Fan-tastic. She's almost done with her master's and then I can finally pop the question."

"You're getting engaged? That's incredible. Congratulations, Sal! Give Angelica a hug for me."

"I will. That's the only way you'll have your arms wrapped around my woman." We both laugh. "But anyway, I haven't heard anything specific, just chatter about some options coming in for both trades and being moved up."

"Anything on pitchers?" I ask already knowing the answer.

"Of course, but isn't there always?"

Groaning, I mutter, "Yeah." Taking one hand from the wheel, I run it through my hair and drop it back to the leather.

"Just because Joey called you out of the blue, that doesn't mean you're being traded. He's an asshole."

"Yeah, but he had his reasons and it wasn't just to check on me. He's the opposite of sunshine and roses."

Chuckling, he advises, "Don't worry about it. He's not worth it. Take a break and go out and find a beautiful woman to let off some steam."

"I have one of those and I don't want another."

"Well, shit. You should've started with that. What's her name?"

"Layla Romano. She's Gabe Romano's younger sister."

"Gabe Romano? Are you fraternizing with the enemy," he teases.

"We were actually set up on a blind date by my aunt and her book club."

"Seriously?"

I laugh. "Yeah, and I was an ass, but she gave me a second chance that I wasn't about to waste."

"You really like her?"

"Damn right I do. There's no one like her."

"I'm happy for you man, but we'll have to agree to disagree," he says, obviously referring to Angelica.

"Fine by me."

"Listen, I'll keep an ear out for you and let you know if I hear anything in the cacophony of the management."

"Thanks, Sal."

"You got it. I gotta go. I'm making Angelica dinner tonight, so I've got my work cut out for me."

"Good luck."

"Thanks. Later, Brennan."

"Bye."

The call disconnects just as I drive into the parking lot at the training facility, ready to hit and throw some balls. I need to ramp things up.

Chapter 32

Layla

Looking at the yellow mums in an acorn planter, I smile, sending a quick text to Levi.

> Thank you for the mums. Moving from cut flowers to plants so they'll last longer?

> Apparently they're perfect for the season.

> Thanks. I like them.

> Are you coming over tonight.

> If you would like me to.

Walking towards the couch, I sit down, calling for my brother. "Gabe, are you coming out of the bedroom sometime in this century?"

Opening the door, he steps out, "Jeez, you're in a hurry."

"I'm not, but I just told Levi I was coming over after I talked to you, so I thought we could actually have a conversation about mom so I know what's going on."

"All right, fine. So, I like two of the places that I looked at for mom and they are both about the same distance from my home base in Oregon," Gabe informs me as he strides into the room and drops down on the couch.

"That's nowhere near Love Canyon."

He scoffs. "Of course not, what the hell do you think I've been doing? We talked about this. I looked all over, Layla. You knew that it was likely we would have to move her near me. Did you forget about that part of our conversation or are you purposely ignoring it?" he inquires sarcastically.

My eyes narrow, but I don't comment because he's right. I was hoping it wouldn't happen. "Okay, so what does that mean?" I ask although I already know the answers. It's the decisions I'm not quite sure about yet.

"There's nothing here. Either there's a waiting list to get in or it's a shit facility that we wouldn't want her in or she's too young to get in. The smart thing is for her to come to Oregon where she'll be close to me instead of someplace where there's no one around. I'd like it if you would come too. I know we both would."

"How am I supposed to do that? I don't have a job there."

"You know you could get one. You're smart, Layla. Plus, your background and experience is fantastic. I'm sure there are places who need a good physical therapist , someone who is great with athletes. I thought you were going to look for something," he says as more of an accusation.

The thought of actually moving and not having a home to come back to makes me anxious, but also excited. It's a lot to think about now that it's not just a possibility, but likely.

Where would I even start? "I could look and see if there's something that works for me."

Gabe leans forward, watching me close. "Let me mention your name to coach. Maybe we can get him to pass your information on." My eyes widen and he quickly amends, "We should get ahead of this, just in case we're able to get mom into one of these places."

"I don't want any favors or special treatment, Gabe."

"You wouldn't get any, but I just found out we are definitely getting two new physical therapists for next season. Maxim was fired and Holden retired."

"Gabe," I say his name in warning.

"It's a position you would have to earn, but it's available. Why wouldn't you put in for it? You're smart and you work hard. Anyone who knows you would say that's an understatement. As for me," he begins, smirking and pointing to himself, "I don't have the kind of power you're giving me credit for, Sis."

I snort making him chuckle. Then, I take a moment staring at him, assessing him. "You would really want to work with your little sister?" I ask only half teasing.

"Actually, yeah, Layla. I've always admired the way you watch players and know exactly what needs to be done to help them be better or heal when they're hurt. You do that for all athletes really. It's incredible. You're smarter and more talented than the two guys that are now gone put together."

"I don't know if I believe that but okay," I concede, joking. A small smile lights up my face and tears form behind my eyelids, but I refuse to let them fall. It's not often I hear a compliment like that from my brother.

Chuckling, he tries brushing it off and asks, "So, does that mean you're okay with me talking to my coach?"

"Sure. Okay. Fine. Yeah, you can mention my name to your coach, but that's it! Please don't push me down their throats."

A sad smile curls his lips. "Got it. Get your resumé ready. You're going to need it."

A dark thought crosses my mind, turning my stomach. Frowning, I question, "I wouldn't have to work with Cal, would I?"

He chuckles, getting a mischievous look on his face. "I'm sure your ex would steer clear and use one of the other therapists if necessary."

I give him a sidelong glance, not sure if I want to know what he's actually thinking or referring to. It's like he knows something I don't. Maybe I should keep it that way. Knowing is not always better. "What are your plans tonight?"

Grinning, he sits a little straighter and answers, "I've got a date."

"Another one? Same woman?"

"I'm not sure who you're referring to, but no."

I grimace. "Sounds like fun, but I gotta ask, how come I haven't met a single one of your dates since you've been here?"

"Because I haven't found one I like enough–yet."

Heaving a sigh, I shake my head at him as he gets up, walking towards the bathroom. "You're such a jerk."

"They don't think so."

"Ewe," I mutter, scrunching up my nose in disgust, only succeeding in making him laugh. "Just go."

"Say hi to Levi," he calls, before the door closes.

Grabbing my keys and phone, I text Levi on my way out the door.

I'm walking over now.

I slip my phone into my pocket and close the door behind me. My mind races, still unsure of how I should bring this up to Levi. Practicing in my head, I try, *"I know we haven't been dating long, but maybe you'll take a chance on me even though we might be moving to two different states after the holidays?"*

My nose scrunches up in displeasure. Yeah, that would go over real well.

I keep thinking we might not be moving and then it wouldn't be an issue, so why should I bring it up for just a chance it will happen? But every day, the chance of moving becomes more likely.

He should know, but I'm petrified to confess.

"Layla," Levi calls making me jump.

My hand falls to my chest, attempting to calm my racing heartbeat. "You scared the hell out of me."

He drapes his arm over my shoulders and presses a kiss to the top of my head. "If that's the case, then we need to have a serious talk. Someone could've easily snuck up on you."

"Someone did. You."

"I'm serious, Layla. I was coming straight at you and you didn't even see me. You have to be more aware of your surroundings. I don't want anything to happen to you." He squeezes me closer as if protecting me.

"I'm fine, Levi, but I'll be more careful," I add, attempting to placate him.

He gives me a look as if he knows exactly what I'm doing. "Thank you. That's all I ask."

"So, are we going somewhere?" I question.

"We can, but I just couldn't sit still. I wanted to go for a walk, so I thought I'd meet you."

"Everything okay?"

Heaving a sigh, he runs his free hand through his hair and drops it to his side. "Yeah, it's fine. I don't know. I'm sorry I cancelled last night. My manager called and it completely threw me off."

"What did he say?"

"Nothing. He just asked about my arm."

I gasp, panic slamming into me. "Oh, my god. Is he not getting my reports?"

"Easy. It's okay. He's getting your reports."

I'm puzzled for barely a moment and then it hits me. "You think they might trade you."

"Yeah, or something like that anyway, and I hate the unknown."

"Yet, you play baseball for a living."

He smirks, shrugging like it's no big deal. "It's fine. I only have two years left on my contract, so whatever happens it will be all right."

My stomach drops. What if he ends up on the other side of the country? It feels like the universe is working against us. I don't want to add to his stress by telling him I might be leaving too. "Do you mind if we just go back to your place and watch a movie or something?"

"Sure. Are you okay?"

"Yeah, I'm just tired," I claim. Pushing up on my tiptoes, I loop my hand around the back of his neck and tug him close, kissing him.

He stares intently into my eyes and finally agrees. "Okay, let's go."

Chapter 33

Levi

"All your reports from your doctors look good, Levi," Joey informs me of what I already know on a conference call with him and my coach, but that's not what I need to hear from him. "Don't fuck it up."

"Thanks," I mutter, monotone. What a fucking asshole.

Coach heaves a sigh. "What he's trying to say is be smart. Up your training and follow the recommendations from your physical therapist."

Yeah, that's exactly what he was trying to say. I shake my head in distaste. His words were much less eloquent. "Got it, Coach. Thanks."

"No, you're not allowed to have this in writing, Chris," Coach prefaces his statement to my agent.

"Okay," Chris agrees.

Coach continues, "We're not about to let you go if I can help it, Brennan. You're damn good at what you do and we all know it. So, ignore the chatter and the assholes and focus because that's all it is—shit talk."

"Thanks, Coach. I will get it done."

"Good. And Levi?" he prompts.

"Yeah?"

"Happy Thanksgiving. Enjoy your time with your family."

"Thanks. You too. Happy Thanksgiving everyone."

"Happy Thanksgiving," Chris says and Joey echoes.

I disconnect, relief flowing through me and a smile curving my lips. Looking around the room with pumpkins, gourds and leaf decorations, I'm reminded of the day and turn around to join the festivities.

Taking a deep breath, a savory scent of turkey, spices and stuffing hits my nose as I make my way back out to the kitchen. Aunt Miranda stands at the counter prepping for Thanksgiving dinner. Pots, pans, knives, and a feast of food are scattered everywhere in various stages of prep, most of it appearing ready to cook.

Aunt Miranda lifts her gaze as I approach and sit down on a stool at the counter. "Is everything okay, Levi?"

Nodding, I claim, "Yeah, it is. Thanks."

"You sure?" She looks up at me again with a question on her face. Sniffling, she looks back at the onion she's chopping, her eyes starting to water, while she tries not to let her tears fall. "It must be important if they are calling you on Thanksgiving morning to talk business."

"Yeah, you would think, but let's just say I've been stressing about my position with the team when apparently I don't need to."

"That's great news."

I nod. "Definitely. Are Della and Lawson up yet?"

"I heard them moving around, but I haven't seen them yet. They both claim they get up early when they're at their own homes, but I don't believe it." I laugh. "By the way, I've been meaning to ask you what time you told Layla, Gabe and their mom to come over today for dinner?"

"Actually, I told Layla if they wanted to come early and hang out or help, we would be happy to have them."

"Good boy."

"Yeah, they're really looking forward to today," I say, not able to wipe the smile off my face. It feels like things are finally looking up again.

"Looks like you are too."

"Of course, I am. Layla is amazing. You know, I don't think I ever really thanked you for setting us up in the first place."

"You're welcome, but I'm just glad you got off your high horse and treated her like she should've been treated all along."

"So am I Aunt Miranda. so am I."

A knock sounds at the door and my smile widens. "I've got it, Uncle Steve calls from the foyer. "Happy Thanksgiving," he greets, Layla's voice ringing clear among the others, my heart full.

She walks in with her mom behind her, followed by Gabe, everyone wishing each other, "Happy Thanksgiving."

Leaning towards Layla, I give her a sweet kiss as she sets an apple pie on the counter. "Hi. I'm glad you're here."

"Thanks for inviting us. I brought you apple pie since you said it was your favorite." Yum.

"Yes, thank you for having us," Gabe says to Aunt Miranda as he sets down two bottles of wine.

"I'm happy to have more people to cook for with my family all at their in-laws houses this year," Aunt Miranda proclaims.

Gabe glances at me, and shakes my hand, smirking. "I can't believe I'm having Thanksgiving dinner with a Lion."

Chuckling, I reply, "I could say the same about you."

"I'm not a Lion."

Shaking my head, I laugh harder.

"We can still kick you out for not being a Lion fan, or at least a fan of my nephew," Uncle Steve teases, standing next to me.

Gabe chuckles, running his hand over his jaw. "I never said I wasn't a fan of Levi...as long as he keeps treating Layla well."

Layla smiles watching us. "All right. Play nice." She shakes her head. "I didn't notice before, but you two really look alike."

I glance at my uncle, grinning. "Yeah, our side of the family has strong genes."

Lawson walks in, his blue eyes the only difference between the two of us. "People used to confuse us as brothers or even twins when we were growing up," he says, jumping right into the conversation. I always loved those moments. They're the kind of family I wanted to be associated with instead of my own. Lawson looks at Layla first and holds out his hand, a crooked smile on his face. "Hi, you must be Layla." She nods and shakes his hand. "I'm this guy's cousin, Lawson."

"It's great to finally meet you." Pausing, she gestures to her mom, "That's my mom and this is my brother Gabe."

He glances at Gabe and shakes his hand. "Yeah, I know who you are. You have a great arm."

"Thanks."

Della walks in soon after and the introductions start again. She looks more like her mom, petite with light brown hair, and her dad's golden brown eyes.

"Can we help with something?" Layla inquires.

"I think I've got it under control. Thank you," Aunt Miranda replies.

I look around the kitchen, taking it all in, feeling a little overwhelmed. Wrapping my arm around Layla, I press a kiss to her head and smile. This is how holidays should be all the people I love in one place.

My heart skips a beat at my internal admission. I don't know if I'm in love, but I'm definitely falling for this woman. This intense feeling is more than it has ever been, but surprising myself, I welcome it.

Thinking about what happens in a couple of months scares the shit out of me, but for now, I'll focus on this. Us. Her.

Reaching down, I tip Layla's chin up and whisper, "I'm thankful for you. Happy Thanksgiving." Closing the distance between us, I press my lips to hers, kissing her tenderly.

"Enough already," Gabe grumbles.

Layla pulls back, blushing fiercely making me chuckle. Looking back at me, she holds my gaze, "I'm grateful for you too, Levi."

My heart clenches, full.

Chapter 34

Layla

The week after Thanksgiving, I walk in from my mom's feeling drained and hungry, trudging towards the kitchen. Involuntarily, my eyes close and I inhale deeply. "Mm, what are you making? It smells so good."

My eyes flutter open, my gaze landing on Gabe standing at the stove, stirring something that smells of tomatoes, onions, and garlic. He smirks, turning off the burner. "I made chili. I figured it would be enough for us for dinner and something we could bring to mom, even freeze some."

"That was a great idea."

"It's ready. Do you want some?"

"Hell, yes," I reply, immediately grabbing bowls from the cabinets making Gabe laugh.

He fills the bowls, his with more than twice as much and carries them to the table while I grab spoons and water for both of us. "Hope you like it," he says as we sit down across from each other.

The bowl is filled with chucks of beef, tomatoes, onions, peppers, corn, black beans, and more. Blowing on my spoon to cool it,

I take a bite, savoring the flavorful dish. "This is delicious, Gabe. Where did you learn how to make this?"

He gives me a bashful shrug, but explains, "I took mom's old recipe a few years back and I've been playing with it to make it mine."

"I'm impressed."

"Thanks." He pauses, taking a bite and asks, "Are you not hanging out with Levi tonight?"

"No, he's at the training facility and I have to work in the morning. Besides, it's been a long day."

"How was mom today?"

"Today was a good day for her," I say, grateful it's true.

He sighs in relief. "Good."

"But I cleaned for her and did her laundry today. Then, I ran to the grocery store and made her something to eat. I was too tired to stay for dinner, so walking into this is like heaven."

A smile tugs at his lips. "I'm glad you're enjoying it."

"That I am."

"Oh, before I forget, the Mavericks' Head Athletic Trainer asked to see your resumé."

I gasp, dropping my spoon back into my bowl, looking at my brother in shock. "What?"

He glances at me, unimpressed. "You heard me."

"What do I do?"

Arching his brow, he states, "You give me your damn resumé so I can forward it to him."

Shaking my head, I stammer, "Yeah, of course, I just mean..."

"I know what you mean." Placing his spoon in the empty bowl, he leans back and crosses his arms over his chest, looking at me. "Did you tell Levi?"

Wincing, I shake my head, and claim, "Not yet."

He huffs a humorless laugh. "Why not, Layla? We've been looking at places for mom for a long time now. You know there's a huge possibility you'll move even if this job doesn't pan out. Don't you think you should tell the guy you're dating? He already lives in a different state for a lot of the year."

My stomach twists, my thoughts in chaos. I know he's right, but it doesn't feel like we're solid enough to tell him I might be leaving. Wouldn't that just cause him to pull away from me? I don't know if I'm ready to do that. Getting my heart involved was a bad idea. "No. There's nothing to tell."

He scoffs. "I'm not sure he'd see it that way."

"If I get a job offer, then there would be something to tell him, but this is just them asking to see a piece of paper and read a few facts. It's not even an introduction nor a conversation, Gabe. It means nothing."

He scoffs, his disappointment written all over his face. "Until it's something, Layla. Even if it's not this, eventually it will be something. That's when you will regret not telling Levi sooner. You know you will."

Tingles prickle my insides, my anxiety spiking. Swallowing, I attempt to gulp them away to no avail. "Don't Gabe. It hasn't happened yet. Besides, it's not like that," I argue irrationally.

Arching his eyebrow in challenge, he questions, "Then, what's it like, Layla? You guys are dating, right? Because he sure as fuck seems to be way into you." My heart lurches at his words. Is that what he thinks? "We spent Thanksgiving with his family for fuck's sake," he emphasizes as if answering my internal question.

"I know, Gabe, I know. Yeah, he's my boyfriend," I admit for the first time out loud. My cheeks darken and a smile curls my lips, despite the conversation.

"Then, what the hell is holding you back?"

Shaking my head, I grumble, "I don't know. Nothing."

"You and I both know that something is because you don't keep secrets like that from people you care about."

He's right, but I don't want to talk about it, about him. "It's not a secret, it's just..." I'm afraid telling him will change everything before we even have a chance to begin and I really like him. Then again, I wouldn't have this doubt or hesitation consuming my thoughts if it wasn't for our father. Especially when I think about all the red flags Levi threw up when I first met him.

His gaze softens, a look of understanding settling over his features. "Don't let dad fuck this up too." I flinch, his aim precise. He deciphered what's going on in my head before I did. "Dad has done enough to ruin things for us, don't you think?" I gulp down the lump in my throat. "Tell Levi," he insists, emphasizing each word. "Sooner rather than later."

I nod, my heart lodging itself in my throat, my anxiety rising. "Yeah, okay, you're right. I will."

Sighing, he offers me a comforting smile. "You know I just want what's best for you."

"I know. Thanks, Gabe."

"I'd get up to hug you, but I'm not ready to move yet. I ate way too fast and I'm so full."

"Gee, thanks." I laugh.

"Well, whoever made this is a damn good cook. I couldn't seem to help myself." He chuckles, amused by his own joke.

"He has a gigantic ego too."

He grins. "Does it matter if it's true?" I giggle, shaking my head in amusement. "I love you, Sis."

"I love you too, Gabe."

"Now, go shower," he says tossing a pillow at me I swiftly deflect. "You really do stink."

Laughing, I walk down the hall, mulling his words over in my head with every step. I know he's right about talking to Levi, so I just need to do it, no matter the consequences.

Chapter 35

Layla

"I'm so happy we're having a girls day today." I grin, holding the glass door at the mall entrance open for Chloe.

"Me too. Now that I'm finally in Love Canyon full time, I barely ever get to see you," Chloe complains, linking her arm through mine as we walk over the white tile floors.

"What about right now?"

"Of course, but we had to drive a few towns over to get away from everything else going on. The only place we've been able to spend time at together recently is at book club."

"Guess we need more book club." I joke and we both laugh. "I know I've been MIA, I'm sorry."

"Please, don't apologize. You have so much going on, especially with your mom, but I miss hanging out with you."

"I miss you too, Chloe."

"How is your mom doing?"

"Okay, I think. I'm grateful Gabe is home."

"But he goes back in two months?"

"Yeah." I attempt to gulp down the sudden lump in my throat.

Chloe stopes, drawing my attention. "No matter what happens, it will be okay–eventually."

"You know, with my mom sick, I hate my dad so much more. I can't help but wonder if maybe he stayed if this would be happening."

"Oh, Layla," she murmurs my name, full of empathy.

"Irrational, right? Or if he was here, maybe he could take some of the weight off Gabe and me and help care for her, but then I'm mad at myself for even thinking that. I wouldn't wish him on my worst enemy."

"It's okay to feel that way. We all agree she's way too young for this to be happening to any of you."

"Thanks," I say giving her a sad smile.

"I'm not placating you, Layla, you know I mean it."

So, after some Christmas shopping, we'll grab dinner and wine closer to home so we don't have to drive later. Plus, Scotty asked if we wanted to meet up after dinner if that's okay with you?"

"Sounds like a plan."

"Have you talked to Levi about the possibility of moving yet?"

"Not you too," I whine.

She arches her eyebrow in question. "Me too?"

"Gabe. He keeps insisting but every time I open my mouth to say something, I clam up. I'm afraid of pushing him away for something that might never happen, especially with how we got started."

"So that's a no. Wouldn't how you got started be a reason alone to tell him? You don't want to spring it on him, Layla."

"No, but what if I never have to tell him?" My face scrunches up knowing how childish I sound.

"I'm pretty sure we both know that won't be the case. Maybe you need a little of me in you so you can just blurt everything out there at once like verbal diarrhea." I snort. "You laugh, but seriously it could do you some good."

"You're probably right, but what am I supposed to say?"

"The truth."

Heaving a sigh, we step into a Christmas store filled with ornaments, considering each one. "Look at this," I say, picking up a lion dressed as a baseball player. "This is adorable. I have to get it for Levi."

"See, you can't stop thinking about him or wanting to do things for him. You've got it bad for him. Yes, I'm probably the worst one to give any advice regarding men, but–"

"Why?" I interrupt. "You have Beck."

She rolls her eyes. "You know me better than anyone, Layla. Do you really need to ask that question?"

We giggle and I insist, "He's damn lucky to have you."

"Anyway..."

"What advice were you going to give me?" I prompt.

"Oh, yeah. You were the one who told me you couldn't date someone who wasn't honest. Is that fair when you can't be honest with him?"

I groan, suddenly dragging my feet. "I'm not lying to him."

"No, but you're holding too much back to claim you're being open and honest with him too."

My eyes narrow at her, but it's not her I'm mad at. "Why do you always have to be right?"

"That's not the first time I've heard those words, and I know it won't be the last," she pauses, smirking, "but I do enjoy hearing them every single time."

I huff a laugh. "You're lucky I love you." Holding up the ornament, I tell her, "I'm getting this for Levi. I'll be right back."

On my way to the counter, I spot one with a black momma bear cuddling her two little bear cubs. Claiming it for my mom, I carefully remove it from the tree and make my way to pay for both of them at the register.

Chloe and Gabe are both right, it's time to step out of my comfort zone and talk to Levi before it's too late.

"Why the hell is Levi Brennan still dating Layla? He's so hot and she's just…plain," the woman finishes, the same woman that used to torture me growing up, with a shrill voice I will never forget. Getting older seems to have made it worse or I'm just more sensitive to it–to her and her friends.

I spotted her almost immediately and attempted to ignore her, pretending I didn't but hearing my name as we walk by makes my footsteps falter, mirroring my heartbeat.

"What's wrong?" Chloe asks, her eyes falling on Sacha and Rachel browsing women's lingerie in the store behind me. "Oh." She frowns.

"We have to get him to come out to the bar one night without her, I bet we could get him to change his mind."

My stomach drops and I grab Chloe's arm for support, my fingers unconsciously digging in. "Ease up there, Supergirl."

"Sorry," I mutter doing as she asks. She's about to drag me away when their next words halt our footsteps.

"When I get a few drinks in him, I'll just seduce him. Once I'm in his bed, he won't be able to remember her name."

Spinning on my heel, I stalk over to them, Chloe on my heels. "You're still talking about other women? Don't you get sick of being a bully?" Chloe accuses.

"It's okay, Chloe. I got this."

Rachel sticks out her hip and arches her eyebrows, looking down on me as if I were the dirt beneath her Jimmy Choo's. "What do you think you got?" she scoffs.

"I've got Levi because he wants a woman who not only respects him but also respects herself enough to show some class. He wouldn't stoop so low."

She laughs like what I said is funny. "You're just a temporary fixation. As soon as the season starts up again, he'll go back to being the player he always was."

Chloe tugs on my arm. "Come on, Layla. Like you said, they aren't worth it."

My heart lodges itself in my throat, their words making an impact and infesting my thoughts, their poison spreading like the plague. Allowing Chloe to pull me far away from them, she finally stops and turns to me. "Do not let them sink their ugly teeth into your brain. They are wrong. Levi is crazy about you."

"But what if they're not?" I ask, my voice trembling.

She shakes her head and puts her arm over my shoulders in support. "If by some ridiculous cosmic force, they're not wrong," she says dramatically and then her voice softens, "he doesn't deserve you. But I don't believe it. He would be a fool not to love you."

"He doesn't love me," I deny, my heart skipping a beat.

"Yes, he does, but you'll know soon enough," she claims.

Even holding myself back a little bit, I've been falling for him, but could he truly love me?

Chapter 36

Layla

Rushing around my kitchen, my hips sway to the light jazz as I hurry to set the table with simple white dishes and black and white patterned placemats. I want everything to be perfect. Tonight, I need to let go of my worry and talk to Levi. There's no more procrastinating. I got the job with the Mavericks. My stomach churns, terrified he'll walk away when I'm already falling for him. The skirt of my black dress adorned with white polka dots swishes by my knees as I hurry knowing he will be here any minute.

A knock at the door stops me in my tracks and I spin around, my ponytail slapping me in the face. Pausing at the mirror, I reassess my appearance, tugging at the straps on the top of my outfit, a halter, hooking at the back of my neck. Quickly, I reapply my red lipstick and pucker my lips.

"Coming," I call, my bare feet slapping against the wood floor as I run to the door.

Yanking the door open, I look up at Levi, dressed in faded jeans and a dark green V-neck shirt and smile. "Hi."

"Wow, Layla, you look gorgeous."

"You're so sweet," I say, feeling my cheeks warm. "Come in."

As I move back from the door, he grips my waist and pulls my body flush to his, sealing his lips over mine. Trailing his fingers up my side, to my jaw, he holds me in place his mouth gliding, in a tender caress.

Breaking the kiss, I gasp for breath at the unexpected but welcome onslaught. Looking into my eyes, he gives me a crooked smile. "Sorry. I couldn't help myself. You wore this dress on purpose didn't you?" he asks eliciting a giggle.

"Dinner is almost ready. I'm not the best cook, but I do okay."

He inhales deeply. "What are we having? Fish? It smells delicious."

"Thank you. Yes, you're right. I made salmon with rice pilaf and sautéed broccoli and garlic. Why don't you sit down at the table and I'll bring it out," I suggest, nibbling on my lower lip.

"Let me help you."

I shake my head. "Not today. I want to do this for you. You've made me so many meals and I've helped you with a few, but it's my turn this time."

Grinning, he agrees, "Okay, I enjoy doing things for you though. You don't ever owe me anything."

"I know."

"How about I'll stay here for a kiss."

I snort and cover my mouth. "Sorry."

"Don't apologize. I love your laugh," he claims, only making me laugh harder. "It's cute."

Pushing up on my tiptoes, I give him a chaste kiss. "There's your kiss," I taunt, spinning away.

Chuckling, he says, "That's not nearly enough."

The buzzer goes off on the oven. "Too bad. You're going to have to wait. I'm not about to let dinner burn."

A few minutes later, I return to the table, setting a plate in front of him and another directly across the table. "This looks and smells incredible, Layla." I sit down, watching him as he takes a bite, his eyes lighting up. "Wow, this is so good."

"I'm glad you like it."

"Thank you. Can I ask what the special occasion is?"

"Does it have to be a special occasion to do something nice?"

"No, it's better when it's not." My stomach twists at his words. "So, where is your brother tonight?" he asks, giving me a reprieve.

"He went to Las Vegas for the night."

"Seriously?" He arches his eyebrows in surprise.

"Yeah, he's meeting up with a couple of his teammates."

"So, I have you for the entire night without the risk of someone walking in on us?"

My cheeks flush, and I swallow the salmon in my mouth. "I guess you could say that."

We finish eating and he steps around the table, holding out his hand. "Dance with me?"

"What?"

"You have music on. Dance with me, please."

I grasp his hand and he playfully jerks me into him. Laughing, I stumble forward. His palm splays across my back, his pinkie dusting my ass. My hand rests on his hard chest, the feel of his thundering heartbeat causing my fingers to tingle.

We sway back and forth, pinpricks spreading across my skin and my chest tight. When I'm close to him like this, it's hard to focus on anything but how I'm feeling. He spins me around and brings me back to him once again.

Reaching up, his hand gently grips my ponytail, tilting my head back until I meet his smoldering gaze. He lowers his head, eliminating the space between us. Our mouths move in time with the music and I melt into him. Gasping, he breaks our kiss. His lips trail down my neck giving me goosebumps.

"Levi," I whimper, "I want you."

Suddenly releasing my hair, his arm zips down my back to my knees and he scoops me up, sweeping me into his arms. I squeal and he chuckles over my mouth. "I'm taking you to your room." His lips come back to mine and he kisses me as he strides down the hall into my bedroom.

Laying me on the bed, he looks down at me full of desire. Reaching back with one arm, he grasps his shirt and yanks it over his head, tossing it on the floor. "You look gorgeous in this dress, but I want to worship you out of it."

My breathing picks up its pace and I beg, "Please."

Rising to my knees, his head falls to the crook of my neck and he places open mouth kisses along my collarbone while he unhooks my dress at the back of my neck. Grazing his hands down my back, he finds the short zipper and slowly drags it down. Letting go of the dress, it drops to the bed, pooling around my knees and leaving me in nothing except my black, lace thong.

He exhales harshly. "You're absolutely breathtaking." Pulling me close, his body covers mine, his hard shaft pressing into my belly. Laying me down, he slides my dress off the rest of the way and drops it to the floor. He crawls over me, my hands wandering over the lines of his muscles from his chest and down his abs. "I have it on authority that I'm cleared for all activities."

"You're cleared, huh?"

"Mm-hm," he hums. His tongue juts out, licking my neck in the spot behind my ear that drives me wild. Moving down, he kisses my collarbone, continuing on to my breast, his teeth grazing my nipple. "Ah, Levi." Arching towards him, my body prickles, coming alive. "I want...I need..." I pant.

"I know baby, I've got you."

One hand covers my breast, kneading and then, pinching my already pert nipple between his fingers. At the same, his mouth covers my other breast. His tongue swirls around my nipple, flicking it before he sucks it into his mouth, slowly releasing it.

My hands continue roaming his body as he switches, giving the other breast the same treatment with both his mouth and hand. Releasing me with a pop, he licks and kisses his way over my belly, along my thigh and nibbling over my sex, his hot breath causing my juices to flow, soaking my thong before he removes it completely and tosses it on the floor.

Sticking his tongue out, he firmly glides it along my slit, my body nearly bucking off the bed. "Ahh!"

"Fuck, you're so sensitive tonight." He licks me again, gently sucking my clit into his mouth. Releasing it, his tongue moves in slow circles around my clit, down my folds and back up to my bud circling it once again. The slow, firm licking, circling and sucking has my body on fire. Both my hands weave into his hair and gently tug him towards my pussy, but he can't get any closer. Instead, he continues the leisurely, methodical, repetitive assault on my pussy.

Breathless I gasp louder, pleading, "Levi, please. Don't stop."

Reaching up, he pinches and rolls my nipples, while he feasts on my pussy. Burning deep in my belly spreads like wildfire, my insides swelling and tingling. Grasping his hair, I scream his name as I explode on his tongue. "Levi!"

Grabbing his pants, he slides a condom out of the pocket and drops them to the floor. Ripping the wrapper, he rolls it on, staring at me, watching me as he licks his lips. Climbing over me once again, he stares down at me, hovering at my entrance. "Are you ready?"

I nod and he plunges inside me in one move, filling me up and making me gasp. My walls squeeze his cock, instantly reigniting my desire. My body thrums with awareness and I know it won't take much to drive me over the edge a second time. "I need you to move," I beg.

Pushing up on his arms, he looks down on me and holds my gaze as he rolls his hips slow, and diving deep, hitting the back of my pussy. I arch my back to meet every thrust, our bodies gliding in a slow dance. My breathing picks up and my insides wrap around him like a glove. Every lunge, and every circle of his hips towards mine has me desperate. His intense gaze, his cock, his rigid body, his kiss, it's all too much, but I want all of it and more.

Increasing his pace, he slides into my hot, wet pussy, skin slapping on skin, both of us gasping. Both of my hands slap his ass and squeeze as if yanking him towards me and urging him to come inside.

My eyes blur and I struggle to breathe, feeling like I'm about to burst. "More, Levi," I beg and he impossibly does as I ask, harder and faster, my insides sparking and taking me to the edge and letting me fall. "Levi," I whimper, finally letting go, my pussy squeezing him as I feel him reaching his climax, his eyes never leaving mine until he can't take it anymore and they flutter closed.

"Fuck, Layla," he mutters, pounding into me, my walls clenching, milking him. He finally collapses, dropping his head to my chest making me realize my fingers are still grasping his hair. Loosening my hold, my hands smooth down his hair.

Lifting his head, he looks at me and grins. "I'm going to go clean up. I'll be right back." He slides out and I immediately feel the loss.

Returning quickly, he lays on the bed and gathers me into his arms, both of us breathless. Running his hand up and down my back, a smile curves his lips as he whispers, "I love you, Layla."

Chapter 37

Levi

Her body stiffens in my arms. I just confessed my love to her and I hear nothing but silence causing my breath to cease. I think that says a lot, but maybe I'm over thinking it. This could be too fast.

Clearing my throat, I change the subject, "I'm excited to spend the holidays together."

"Yeah, me too," she murmurs, her unenthusiastic response clutching my heart.

Shit.

"What about after the holidays? Do you have anything you want to do in the new year?"

"Levi." The way she says my name soft and tender gives me goosebumps. Her hand falls to my chest, over my racing heart-beat like she has done so many times. "I'm falling for you too." Her words send my heart soaring and the tension easing out of me. It's not the same as my declaration, but it's heading in that direction. "But we need to start talking about what happens after the holidays. I can't stop thinking about it," she emphasizes, her voice defeated as she looks away.

My hand cups the back of her neck, my thumb caressing the back of her jaw, needing her to look at me. "We can figure it out. If we want this to work, we make it work."

"You go back to Vegas in a couple months. Then what?"

"Then, come with me to Las Vegas." The words are out before I even think about it and when they do, I recognize that it is exactly what I want.

I want her with me.

She shakes her head. "I can't."

A hopeful smile tugs at my lips. "Yes, you can. You can move in with me. If you're not ready for that, I do understand, I know some places that I think you would like and we can find a place for your mom."

Wincing, she whispers, "Levi, no," her voice strained.

Hoping I can find a way for her to agree, I continue adding reasons this will work. "You can find a job there. You're so fucking smart, Layla, I know you could find something you love. And I know you don't want my help, but I can give you a recommendation or something as one of your patients. We can figure it out, but at least we'll be together."

Her eyes well and a tear escapes. "No, Levi, I can't," she says a little louder.

The way she says it makes me hesitate. I look at her again with confusion in my eyes, and force out the question, I don't know if I want the answer to. "What do you mean, you can't?"

"I mean I can't go to Las Vegas with you. Gabe found a place in Oregon for my mom near him."

"Okay," I say, dragging out the word. "That would be hard, but that doesn't mean–"

"I'm going with them," she interrupts.

"What?" I gasp in shock.

"I need to be near them with everything my mom is going through. Gabe and I need to both be there for her and for each other."

My head falls back in humorless laughter. Is she fucking kidding me? "Were you ever planning on telling me?"

"Levi," she says my name quiet, apologetic. But I don't want her useless regret. Fuck that.

"You must've known before now, right? A decision to move isn't something that happens overnight."

"I didn't think it would happen at all or I was in denial. I'm not sure."

My jaw clenches and I nod, processing her words. She knew and didn't trust me enough to even talk to me about it. A lump forms in my throat. Clearing it, I ask, "But it's a done deal?"

She flinches and croaks, "Yeah."

"Have you started looking for a job in Oregon?"

Her face flushes and my heart plummets, knowing even before the words leave her mouth. "I was offered a position as one of the Maverick's physical therapists next season. I start at the end of February."

"Fuck me," I mutter under my breath. She reaches for me, her hand falling to my shoulder and I flinch away, her silence feeling like a betrayal. Climbing out of bed, I yank my jeans on feeling like my world is suddenly out of control.

"You know when we met, you were so insistent about being open and honest or this would never work, yet you don't even bother telling me about this, something that is going to alter your entire future," I emphasize, her betrayal slamming into me like a freight train. "Didn't you think that this might impact me even a little bit, no matter what your decision would be?"

"I...I..." she stammers.

"Fuck, Layla. I would've been there for you to support you. I'm not the guy who will make a decision for you. I want what you want, no matter what it is. You should know that about me by now." Pausing, I shake my head in disbelief. Pointing to myself, I glare, insisting, "I deserved to be a part of the fucking conversation!"

"I'm sorry," she whimpers, tears streaming down her cheeks, appearing heartbroken. It hurts me to see her this way, but she doesn't understand how heartbreak truly feels or she would've talked to me.

I don't have the capacity to comfort her right now. Not when she's the one who deceived me.

Shaking my head, I step back, struggling to breathe and to process. "I can't do this right now. I'm sorry Layla, but I can't believe you would keep this from me. You made the decision to keep this from me. I've always said you're a smart woman, so I know you understand the concept of omission is the same as lying. *You lied to me.* I need time to think."

"Levi, I'm sorry," she cries. Her apology feels hollow, no matter how desperate she sounds--like another betrayal.

Grabbing my shirt off the floor, I yank it on and step into my shoes, striding for the front door without a backwards glance.

Chapter 38

Layla

I curl up on the couch and stare blankly at the Christmas tree sitting in the corner of my living room with tears in my eyes. The holiday came and went without anything more than a simple text from Levi, wishing me a Merry Christmas, but it was anything but merry. I cried myself to sleep, my heart aching and filled with regret.

Gabe walks in the front door and shakes his head when he spots me. Stomping towards me, he flops onto the couch by my feet with a heavy sigh. "You fucked up, Layla. Apologize."

"I know I did and I already did. Many times."

"Not to his face since the day he walked out. An *I'm sorry* text to someone who betrayed you is like a punch in the face."

My gaze narrows on him. "Not helping," I grumble.

"Women always want a genuine apology face to face. Men want that too and Levi deserves it. He asked for time and he's had it. Stop sulking, clean your ass up and go beg for his forgiveness."

Tears blur my vision and I ask, my voice barely a whisper, "What if he doesn't forgive me?"

"You can't live in fear Layla, you're stronger than that. And I think he meant it when he said he needed time. You forgave him for being a dick, now it's his turn to do the same for you. But if you don't ever take a chance, you'll never know if you missed out on what your life should've been."

Forcing myself to move, I mumble my appreciation as I head for the shower, "Thank you, Gabe."

An hour later I'm standing in front of Levi's place dressed in a white skirt and a basic red polo with an apple pie in my trembling hands, scared out of my mind. Taking a deep breath, I raise my hand and knock. Barely a moment later, Levi yanks the door open and freezes.

My breath hitches as I stare at him dressed in black net shorts and a white Lions t-shirt, unshaven and his mouth open in surprise. "Layla."

"Hi, Levi. I'm sorry to bother you, but I was really hoping we could talk. May I come in?"

"Um, yeah," he mumbles and scrambles back. "Do you want anything to drink?"

"Maybe water? And I brought you an apple pie."

He huffs and takes it from me. "Thanks, and thanks for the ornament too."

My heart clenches hating the distance between us. He disappears into the kitchen with the pie and returns with a glass of water and handing it to me without a word.

Walking across the room, he sits down in the recliner, where there's no room for me. My heart drops further, losing hope, but now that I'm here, I'm not going to leave without speaking up.

"I'm sorry, Levi. I know those are only words, but I am so sorry. I'm hoping that you'll give me a chance to prove to you just how sorry I am."

He sighs and runs his hand through his hair. "Look, Layla. I get that you're sorry, and that you regret it, but what I'm struggling with the most is the fact that you didn't trust me enough to even have a conversation with me. Now that you feel bad, you suddenly trust me? I don't buy it."

I flinch, understanding washing over me. Sitting down on the couch, I take a sip of water and begin talking. "You're right. It doesn't make sense, but what's crazy is that I already did trust you." He scoffs, but I keep talking. "I couldn't come up with a reasonable solution and I was scared of losing you, so I said nothing at all. I tried to tell you so many times, Levi, but I chickened out every time."

"Layla…"

Needing to explain, I continue, "My experience with a long distance relationship, even temporarily, has been my dad cheating repeatedly on my mom while my mom raised us and everyone worshiped him."

"You know I'm sorry that happened to you, but I'm not him."

"No, you're not, but you were a player in the past. I know it's not fair, but it hurts thinking about all the women you've been with or could be with and when I hear other women talking about you." I flinch at the thought.

"It doesn't matter if I'm not interested. Since I met you, you are all I see."

My heart lurches with hope. "I know, but I struggled a lot growing up. A lot of the girls were not nice to me and if it weren't for Chloe's visits to stay with her Nana, I don't know where I would be. The day before you came over, Chloe and I were Christmas shopping and ran into two women that have done and said some really mean things to me. Because of them, I really struggled with my self-confidence."

"Layla, you're incredible, don't let anyone tell you different."

"It wasn't that. They were talking about you, asking why you were with me and saying they could get you to change your mind. They put it in my head that you would go back to baseball and leave me behind."

"That's not true. I asked you to come with me and you said no."

Sighing, I nod. "Yeah, I did because I need to be there for my mom and my brother. Plus, my career is important to me, but I don't want to take advantage of you like other people have in the past. I want us to be on even ground in our relationship...if we have one. But I really don't want to lose you, Levi. If you give me a chance, I could come visit and we could be together during the off-season. Not just the off-season, but..."

"But we could figure it out," he finishes.

"Yeah," I answer, hopeful.

"I really don't want to give up on us, Layla."

My heart lurches as I suck in a lungful of air, trying not to cry. "Me neither. I love you, Levi."

He gasps, his eyes flaring. "What did you just say?"

"I said I love you, Levi."

"Can you come a little closer? I'm having trouble hearing you from all the way over there."

I giggle, feeling like the weight of the world is being lifted from my shoulders. Crossing the living room, I stand in front of him seated in the chair. Staring into his eyes, I leave my heart open and vulnerable and reiterate, "I love you, Levi."

A smile curves his lips and he pulls me into his lap, making me squeal. "Good because I love you too, Layla." His forehead falls to mine and he whispers, "So damn much." He presses his mouth to mine and kisses me. Sweeping his tongue inside, ours meet, tangling together in a slow dance with my heart full.

Chapter 39

Levi

"You're buying me flowers now?" I give her a crooked smile, looking down at her standing in my doorway, holding a white bouquet between us.

"Well, someone I love once told me that lilies mean forgiveness and although you said you forgave me, it's important to me that you know I'm serious about asking you for it."

A lump forms in my throat and I swiftly clear it, tamping down my emotions. "Smart man," I tease, smirking.

"I never said anything about the person being a man," she claims, not able to keep a straight face.

Laughing, I pick her up and spin her around, taking her inside with me and kicking the door shut. "Now you're in trouble."

"Levi, the flowers," she squeals.

Moving back enough to remove the floral barrier between us, I set them on the table and swing her right back into my chest. "No more flowers. Just me and you."

My palm goes to her cheek, and my thumb glides over her full lips a moment before my mouth crashes down on hers. The laughter instantly dissipates, replaced with pure desire. Her mouth falls open with a breathy moan and my tongue immediately sweeps inside, tangling with hers.

We quickly get lost in each other. My hands roam, gliding over her clothes, her pert nipples straining to break through. Our mouths move in tandem kissing, licking, nibbling, and sucking.

Her hand skates over my chest, down to my hard cock, pushing against the zipper of my jeans, desperate to escape.

Her phone rings, and she breaks the kiss, reaching for it. Inhaling her floral scent, I press my face into her neck as she answers. "Hello?" Pausing, she listens to the caller, while my tongue licks behind her ear.

Grinning, she leans away from me, attempting to focus on the call. "Okay. That's perfect. Thanks!" Disconnecting her phone, she puts it in her pocket and playfully swats at me, giggling. "That was my brother."

"Oh, sorry, about that." I kiss her on the neck again.

She laughs. "No, you're not, but I'm still making you stop."

Straightening, I look down at her, my eyebrows drawn together in disbelief. "Seriously?"

"Yeah, I told you, I have plans for our date tonight," she informs me.

"Can't we just stay in?"

"No, and we have to go or else we're going to be late."

A groan leaves my lips. "Okay. Then, since I know you're looking forward to this, let's go before I beg you to change your mind."

She laughs. "I promise you'll have fun."

"I'll be with you, I know I will."

"That sounds like one of your lines, Mr. Brennan."

Chuckling, I claim, "You are absolutely the only person I would say that to." Until we have kids–the thought crosses my mind before I can stop it, but it doesn't make me shy away.

"Come on, Levi, let's go."

I slide into the passenger seat of Layla's car, her scent wrapping around me like a glove. "Damn, it smells good in here. It's a cute car."

She side-eyes me as she pulls onto the road. "Cute?" I chuckle in response. "I forgot you've never been in my car. It makes you look small," she teases.

Shaking my head in amusement, I inquire, "So where are we headed?"

"You'll find out when we get there."

Grinning, I relax back in the seat, enjoying the sound of her singing along with the radio.

A half-hour later, she's driving into the pro ice hockey arena, the billboard announcing tonight's game.

VALLEY DIAMONDBACKS VS SAVANNAH LEOPARDS

"We're going to a hockey game?"

Shrugging, she explains, "Yeah, I figured you never get to sit and watch a game unless you're working. I thought it would be fun to go to a game where you can enjoy it without having any pressure and it's truly time off together."

My heart clenches. "I can't believe you thought of this. Do you even know if I like hockey?"

She parks the car and looks at me, suddenly nervous. "It was either this or basketball."

My head falls back in laughter. Reaching for her, I palm her neck, my thumb caressing her jaw near her ear. "Yes, I like hockey. This was so damn sweet, Layla. I fucking love you. Doing this," I gesture to the arena behind us. "This is awesome."

"So does that mean you really do forgive me?"

Dropping my forehead to hers, I keep my grip on her neck, exhaling a harsh breath. "You did not have to do something like this, Layla. I forgave you already. Just knowing you were genuinely regretful and you love me, that was more than enough." Taking a deep breath, I attempt to process my thoughts. "Let's make a promise to each other."

"Okay," she whispers.

"From now on, let's do things for each other because we want to."

"Does that mean I'm not getting any more flowers?" she jokes.

Chuckling, I reply, "You'll have so many you can start your own flower shop if you want. I love buying you flowers." Tipping my chin, I kiss her hard. "Let's do things because we love each other."

"Levi, I do love you."

"I know, baby, and that's all I need."

Kissing her again, our mouths move together soft and slow. My tongue juts out, licking the seam of her lips, keeping our kiss tender and light. Breathless, we break our kiss. "Should we go to the game before it's over, or do you just want to make out in the parking lot all night? I'm up for either."

She snorts, blushing as she falls back in her seat looking sexy as fuck. Making out anywhere sounds damn perfect. "Let's go watch a hockey game."

Chapter 40

Layla

Sitting across from Chloe and Beck on the soft, black leather booth, I watch the waitress walk away with our drink order. The savory scent of Italian bread, tomato, basil and garlic fills my nose. The smells seem to be embedded into the pores of this dining room. It's the same aroma I remember from this place as a kid, hitting me with a sense of nostalgia.

"Remember when we were throwing spaghetti up on the chandelier to see if we could hook it?" I ask Chloe.

She laughs. "Oh, my gosh, yes. We said we were trying to decorate it for Halloween." Levi and Beck both laugh. "Weren't we with your parents?"

"And Gabe."

"Oh, yeah, and we tried throwing it every time they looked the other way."

Grinning, I add, "And when Gabe tried, he got caught and got in so much trouble. He was so mad."

We laugh and Levi asks, "Did you two always get in trouble together?"

"No." I shake my head. "We just knew how to laugh together and we read and talked a lot of books."

"It was great when I had to go home. We had our own book club then."

"And now we have a different kind of book club," I say.

"I've definitely become a big fan of the book club," Levi claims, pressing a kiss to my temple and making me blush.

Beck says, "I'm glad we're finally doing this."

"Yeah, I like the stories and I'm glad I'm getting a chance to know the two of you a little better with just the four of us."

"Me too," Chloe and I agree in unison.

My smile waivers, emotion crawling up my throat, attempting to consume my insides. I feel Levi's shift, moving closer. "You okay?" he whispers.

I nod, taking a deep breath, trying to get my emotions under control when they feel like they came from out of nowhere. "I'm just going to miss this and it's only the first time we got to do it."

"It's going to be fine, Layla," Chloe says reaching across the table for my hand.

At the same time, Levi's hand falls to my thigh underneath the table, his fingertips trailing along the bare skin at the edge of my cranberry pencil skirt, trying to soothe me with the simple movement. "She's right," he insists.

"I know. I just don't know how I'm going to say goodbye to you, Chloe," I claim, my voice cracking and tears shining in my eyes.

"Then don't," she demands, vehemently shaking her head.

"You'll be back and I'll come visit you too. It's going to be fine. It will be like it was before, but this time we're adults and we have more control about traveling to see each other. It won't be anything like the summer I had to go home early because I got sick, leaving you with the mean girls and prepubescent boys. You're leaving me with Nana and Beck while you are going to love your new job. Plus, Gabe and your mom will be there." She glances at Levi. "You just have to share some of your Layla phone time with me or I'll come to Vegas and steal your phone. Or maybe all your stuff so you don't know it's me."

A snort escapes before I can stop it. Quickly covering my mouth, I burst out laughing and Beck chuckles. He looks at Chloe, his eyes gleaming with adoration, while Levi sits gaping, looking between the three of us as if we have a secret we're keeping from him. "What just happened?"

"This is the full power of Chloe and me. I couldn't ask for a better best friend." A broad smile lights up my face.

"Okay. Anything that makes you this happy is a good thing in my book," he murmurs, chuckling. "I'm just not going to promise I will always understand what's going on."

Giggling, I lean over, kissing him on the corner of his mouth. "You're adorable, Levi."

"That's just me," Chloe claims, shrugging. We all laugh, the somber mood lightening.

"Yes, you are adorable," Beck adds, his arm falling around her shoulders and giving her a squeeze.

Levi holds up his glass of water, prompting, "A toast?"

We all reach for our glasses and raise them. "To good friends," I say.

"And great loves," Levi adds.

"I'll drink to that," Beck agrees, smiling at Chloe.

The four glasses meet in the middle with a delicate chime. "Cheers," our voices collide and we take a sip.

"Maybe we should get out of here and give them the table," Levi suggests, nodding towards the staff hovering nearby.

I laugh. "I'm pretty sure they're standing there because they recognize you."

Chuckling, he admits, "It's been a while since anyone has said anything. I started to think I was unrecognizable."

Beck scoffs, understanding Levi's frustration. "That never happens, but I wish it did. Although, sometimes when you're in a small town like Love Canyon, they give you the respect you deserve and let you enjoy your personal time. Knowing who to steer clear of helps too."

"I bet."

Levi and Beck, both lay down some cash and we slide out of the booth, waving towards the staff before we walk outside, heading towards our cars.

"Tonight was fun," I say, a lump forming in my throat once again.

Levi's arm goes protectively around my shoulders. "Why don't we do it again next week," he suggests, glancing at me, while a smile in approval lights up my face. It's like he's reading my mind.

"Yes," Chloe agrees, glancing at Beck.

"See you soon," I say, feeling like things really will be okay as I slide into Levi's car. Even when we're not together, the little things he's doing are letting me know that he will be there for me to support me, love me and protect me, even when we can't be together.

The little things like the hand on my back or on me knee, the sweet kiss, or words of support are all telling me that I can trust him. Hopefully, he knows I want to do the same for him.

Isn't that what we all want?

Chapter 41

Levi

The next month flew by. I've spent as much time with Layla as possible, relishing every moment, but today is the day that we both have to leave for preseason in separate states and I fucking hate it.

She clings to me and I hold her tight, neither of us wanting to let go. "I'm going to miss you, so much, Levi."

"I'm going to miss you too, Layla, but I promise, we'll talk every day, even if it's just to say goodnight and good morning, but I don't want to go a day without hearing your voice. No matter how chaotic training is or what's going on, we'll find time to talk. Okay?"

She nods against my chest. "Please, let's try to find that time, Levi. I know I'll be busy learning everything about the facilities, the team, the players, the staff..." she trails off and whimpers.

"And you're going to be amazing. They're damn lucky to have you," I insist, pressing another kiss to her lips.

"All right you two, sorry to break it up, but we gotta go," Gabe says, stepping out of Layla's house, the sold sign still sticking in the front yard. "The house is clear."

"Thanks."

"I'm fucking glad we moved mom out to her new place first. That would've been way too much at once," Gabe complains, smirking at Layla's back when she doesn't move or respond. "Are you ready to go, Sis?"

"No," she mumbles into my chest, her tears dampening my shirt. "I'm going to stay for a while."

Gabe shakes his head, chuckling.

"You're always welcome to come with me."

"Yeah, I know, but I can't."

Although I'm already aware, it still fucking hurts to hear it again. Taking a deep breath, I push my own emotions out of my head and attempt to comfort her. "Yeah, I know, and it's going to be okay. We aren't going to be apart forever. This is only temporary."

"We can do this, Levi." Pushing up on her tiptoes, she kisses me with a hunger that sends a shock of electricity straight through me.

Breaking our kiss, I mumble over her lips, "I'll see you soon, Layla." Nudging her back, I cradle her face in my hands and look into her eyes, sharing my vulnerability. "I love you."

"I love you, too." Her voice cracks and she kisses me again, her lips soft, tears salty, and my chest aching. I didn't know it could hurt this much.

Guiding her towards the car, I open the door, keeping my arm around her until she slips inside. She rolls down the window the moment the door closes. Leaning my head in the window, I kiss her again. Glancing at Gabe, I say as more of a plea, "Take care of her."

He chuckles, both of us knowing he will. "Bye, Levi." He waves.

"I love you," I reiterate, kissing her and hauling my head out of the window as Gabe starts driving away from the curb and taking my heart with him.

Heaving a sigh, I don't take my eyes off the car. Layla sticks her hand out the window and waves, just before they disappear around the corner. I get in my own car and blink back my tears, practically choking on emotion. Taking a deep breath, I attempt to control my breathing and start my car.

Turning in the opposite direction, I drive towards Las Vegas, when all I want to do is follow Layla. My hand goes over my heart as I drive. Rubbing, I try to take the pain away. I didn't know it could hurt like this.

Chapter 42

Layla

Crouching down by the cabinets, I empty the boxes of medical supplies from a recent delivery and try to organize them properly.

"Good morning, Layla." Mr. Zetner calls. I look up as he approaches with a file in his hand.

"Hi, Mr. Zetner," I say, rising off the floor.

"I have to go to the ballfield to help Taylor and Miles with a couple of the players," he says, giving me an apologetic look. "But I have a player coming down now for his leg and I need you to take a look at him for me."

"Of course, no problem," I agree, taking the file.

"Thanks," he mumbles and spins on his heel, jogging out of the room.

Glancing at the file, I see the player only needs me to massage it out, so that should be easy. A moment later, I hear someone behind me. Turning, I gasp, staring into the eyes of my ex-boyfriend. "Cal."

"Layla," he grins, a sly smile curling his lips.

Fuck. I should've looked at the file before I agreed. Please have it be someone else. "What do you want?" I grit through my teeth.

"I pulled a muscle in my leg and coach sent me down here to see Zetner, but I'd much rather see you."

Clenching my fist, I mutter. "Good because I'm apparently what you've got."

He gets a mischievous look in his eyes and saunters to one of the tables and sits on the end. "I'm having trouble with my left leg," he claims, showing me the muscle on the inside of his thigh.

"Are you fucking kidding me?" I blurt out. "You probably got hurt there from all your extracurricular activities."

Arching his brow, he asks, "I said I was sorry, Layla. She took advantage of me when I was drunk. It meant nothing to me."

I huff a humorless laugh. "Do you think that matters to me?"

He pinches his lips tightly together. "So, are you going to help me with my leg or not? I'm happy to go ask your boss for help instead."

"No, no, it's fine."

Gritting my teeth, I begin working on him, cringing as a moan leaves his mouth. Sure, I've heard it before while I'm working, but hearing it from Cal makes me nauseous. "That feels so good, just a little higher."

I dig in harder than necessary, making him flinch and grab my wrist. "What the fuck, babe?"

"Don't call me babe and let me do my job."

He wrenches me closer and my eyes narrow. "Layla, please. I miss you. We were so good together."

"I have a boyfriend. Let me go."

"So, it's true? You're fucking one of the players from the Lions?"

"That's not your business, Cal. Let go of me and let me do my job or get the fuck out."

"I just want to talk, Layla." Glaring at him, I don't respond and he growls in annoyance. "What if I don't want to do those things?"

"Then I'll report you for harassment."

"Hurst? Are you bothering Miss Romano?" Mr. Zetner questions as he reenters the training room.

Cal drops my hand like a child who touched a burning stove. "No, Sir. We're old friends."

"That's not what it looks like to me." Glancing back at me, he says, "Layla, take an extra kit up to the dugout and assist your brother."

"Got it." I grab the first aid kit and practically run out of the training room. My heartrate settles when I finally reach the dugout and spot my brother. Sinking down on the bench near him, my body sags with relief.

Leaning towards my ear, he asks, "You okay?"

Gulping down the lump in my throat I nod, but his furrowed brow remains. He knows me better than that. I'll tell him at the end of the day. I'm not about to piss him off during practice. "Mr. Zetner said you were hurt?"

"Nope, I'm good. Are you sure you're all right?"

A small smile curls my lips. Looks like I have my own team already watching my back. "Yes, Gabe. I'm great."

Chapter 43

Levi

Players move in and out throughout the season and during preseason training this year, there seems to be more shuffling than normal with some last minute trades. My pitching is good, but I'm still not throwing like I was before my injury. It gets better every day. Unfortunately, the new guys they brought in are phenomenal making my stomach turn, feeding my concern. My thoughts drift back to the possibility of a trade, especially knowing I was already on Joey's list. He'd gladly send me somewhere across the country.

Sighing, I massage my shoulder and arm. My muscles are sore as hell and I'd love to jump in the damn shower. Instead, I'm here waiting for one of our trainers. Derek will likely be the one helping me. He's okay, but he's nothing like Layla.

Damn, I miss her.

Grabbing my cell, I dial her number, hoping to hear her voice while I wait. She answers almost instantly, bringing a smile to my face. "Levi, hi."

"Hi, beautiful. I miss you."

"I only have a few minutes, but you called at a good time. How are you calling right now?"

Chuckling, I explain, "I'm waiting for one of the trainers. My arm is a little sore, so they want me to have it looked at."

"You probably need my hands," she teases.

"You have no idea," I groan, imagining her hands on me. Swiftly shaking the thought away, not wanting to get worked up here, I ask, "How's everything going?"

"So much better," she croons. "Apparently, Cal got traded yesterday. I don't know where, but I don't care. I will never have to put my hands on him again."

A smile curves my lips as I breathe a sigh of relief. I knew Gabe was trying to keep him away from Layla, but work is work and it doesn't always happen the way we would like. I wanted to fly up just to pummel that asshole when she told me about him messing with her last week. "That's fantastic news."

"Yeah, I thought so too," she agrees, her happiness evident. I hear someone calling her name in the background. "I'm sorry, Levi, but I gotta get back to work. I love you."

"I love you too."

Heaving a sigh, I disconnect and set my phone down next to me as a player I don't recognize walks up. He looks familiar, but I can't quite place him. Must be one of the new guys. "This is where the training rooms are?" he inquires.

Glancing at him, I nod. "Yeah."

Holding out his hand, he introduces himself, "Just got traded from the Mavericks." My heart stops as I stare at the man who screamed for my attention with only one word, already knowing the name about to spew from his mouth. "Cal Hurst."

Fuck. Layla's asshole ex is my new teammate. I grip his hand a little tighter than I should, his eyes narrowing. "Levi Brennan," I grit my name through my teeth.

He laughs, ripping his hand away. "Got any tips on clubs that like players?" he questions. "I need a night out after the shit week I just went through." Quirking my brow, I remain silent, fisting my hands at my sides to keep myself from doing something stupid, but he keeps fucking talking. "My ex started working on my old team and couldn't keep her hands off me. We get caught and I'm the one that gets traded. The bitch's brother likely helped with that."

"Shut your fucking mouth before I shut it for you," I seethe, my insides bouncing off the walls with unrepressed anger.

A sinister smirk curls Cal's lips telling me he knows exactly who I am and he's intentionally pushing me. "So, you are the Lion I heard is fucking my ex. I don't blame you, she has such a sweet pussy."

I barely register the man himself or the sneer on his face before I swing, two of my teammates yanking me off the dirtbag.

Shit.

Cal Hurst is my new teammate.

When they let me go, I storm down the hall and into coach's office, vibrating with anger. This can't be fucking happening. "I can't work with him Coach."

"Who? What the fuck just happened?" Coach asks, looking up from his desk.

Joey jogs in after me, nudging my shoulder back with barely restrained anger. "What the hell are you doing laying a hand on Cal Hurst? You're the fucking veteran here. You should know better than to hit anyone, let alone a new teammate."

"He's an asshole."

"Does that matter when you're on the same team?"

I shake my head in denial. "No fucking way."

"The fucking ego on you, Brennan. And even you know your numbers aren't back to what they should be after your injury. You're done. Finished!" Spinning on his heel, he storms out of the office just as fast as he flew in.

Coach looks at me and sighs, disappointment shining in his eyes. Running his hand through his thick gray hair he drops it onto his desk. "Shit, Brennan. What the hell were you thinking?"

"I'm sorry Coach, but…"

He holds up his hands to stop me. "Save it Brennan. It doesn't matter. It's done. See the physical therapist and get the fuck out of here." I give him a firm nod. "But come see me first thing in the morning."

"Got it, Coach."

He huffs a humorless laugh and shakes his head in disbelief. "With what I know, maybe this will end up as a gift for you, but you can't take this back."

"If you're talking about Hurst, I don't want to take it back. He deserved it and so much worse."

Ignoring my comment, he says, "Good luck, Levi. See you bright and early." Then, he drops his head, focusing back on his work, dismissing me.

My eyebrows draw down in confusion, but I do as he directed, still fuming.

Cal Hurst is a fucking asshole. I can't believe he was traded here. There's no way I can be civil to that man, especially with what he said to me.

What the fuck am I gonna do?

Chapter 44

Layla

My heart aches reading the recent card Levi sent with beautiful pink tulips. "I miss you, Layla. Love, Levi." It's simply sweet and breaks my damn heart. Sighing, I slip it into my pocket and check my schedule for the day. Today appears to be a lighter day as long as we have no new injuries.

I look around the training room and make sure everything was cleaned and put away last night. We have half a dozen massage or patient tables, weight equipment, bands, parallel bars for leg injuries, medicine balls, rollers, mats, exercise balls a short row of NuStep machines, treadmills, ellipticals and other various exercise and weight machines along with tens units, handheld sonos and more. I've never seen anything so thorough. I have everything I could possibly need to do my job and more. Then on the other end we walk through our medicine and first aid area into a space with ice baths, jacuzzi tubs, and saunas. It's incredible.

"Morning, Layla."

I turn towards the deep voice and smile at my boss. He's a nice guy, a couple inches taller than my brother, with a shaved head and ridiculously strong. He's married with his third baby on the way. "Good morning, Mr. Zetner."

"We have two new trades coming in today. One this morning and one later today. I need you to do their intakes."

"Got it."

"Here's the first," he says handing me the file, "and I'll set the second in your box."

"Thank you."

The first man, Craig, walks in ten minutes later and my day quickly gets away from me.

At the end of the day, Gabe walks in with a tired smile on his face. "Hey Sis. How was your day?"

"Good, but I haven't gotten out of here all day. How about you?"

"Good. I'm going to shower and head over to see mom. Are you done soon?"

"I have one more new intake on a trade and then I'm done."

He nods, the corners of his lips twitching up. "I saw the new guy. Taylor was showing him around. I'm sure he'll be here soon."

"I'll see you later."

"Bye, Gabe." I wave as he backs out of the room.

Shuffling around, I prepare a patient bed and new forms for the intake before making my way to my inbox. Picking up the folder, I look at the name and my heart stops.

"Levi Brennan," I whisper in shock, barely breathing.

"That's me," he says, his deep voice echoing in the now empty room.

Slowly spinning on my heel, the man himself stands in the doorway with a broad smile on his face. Sprinting across the room, I jump into his arms and wrap my legs around his waist as he catches me, laughing.

"Levi," I cry, not able to fight the tears rolling down my cheeks.

He presses his face into my neck and inhales deeply. "Hi, beautiful."

"I guess you two know each other," Taylor mutters. Tearing my face away from Levi's chest, I look at Taylor flipping his dark hair out of his light eyes, full of amusement.

"She's my girlfriend," Levi answers, not bothering to lift his head.

"I sure as hell hope so because we all know she's not available and if you're not him, she's in deep shit."

We all chuckle and I slowly lower my legs to the ground without letting go. "Thanks for bringing him." Taylor nods, taps the door and exits without another word.

"Damn, I missed you," Levi murmurs and presses his lips to mine, kissing me hard, messy, and desperate.

Forcing myself to pull back, I say, "I missed you, too, but how did this happen?"

Levi chuckles darkly. "Let's just say that your ex was apparently good for something." My eyebrows draw down in confusion. "He was traded to the Lions and I got into it with him. And today, I was on a plane to you."

"Wait, you got in a fight with Cal? Are you in trouble with the league?"

"A slap on the wrist. Then, ironically they traded up with the Mavericks and here I am."

"I can't believe it," I murmur, kissing him again.

He chuckles over my lips. "Neither can I."

A throat clearing breaks us apart, followed by a low chuckle. My face burns as I look around Levi, finding my boss. "You two know each other?" he asks, arching his brow in challenge.

"You know I do," I tell him. Glancing at Levi, I add, "I may talk about you a little bit."

My boss laughs. "More than a little. Nice meeting you, Brennan," he adds, holding his hand out for Levi. "I'm the Head Athletic Trainer here, Bill Zetner."

Levi shakes his hand, keeping one hand on me. "Nice meeting you. I'm really happy to be here."

"I can see that and I'm going to go home to see my wife and kids. Layla, after you finish up Levi's intake, you can handle locking up tonight?"

"No problem."

"Great, I'll see you two kids tomorrow," he jokes, waving as he walks out of the training room, shutting the door behind him to give us some privacy.

"I like your boss," Levi says, grinning.

"Me too."

Palming my cheek, Levi kisses me with barely restrained fervor, backing me up towards the training table. It bumps my back when I stop him with a hand on his chest, nudging him back. "Wait."

"What's wrong?" he asks.

"I don't think we should do this here at work."

Disappointment shines in his eyes, but he acquiesces, showing me respect and filling my heart. "If that's what you want, I can wait."

"Take off your shirt and jeans and climb up on the table," I instruct.

Smirking he does as I ask, sitting on the table in black boxer briefs, his thick thighs on display.

My heartbeat becomes erratic as I go through a few basic assessments, every touch to his skin, electric. Struggling to control my breathing, I set the clipboard down next to him, slowly running my hands up his arms, over his shoulders and down his chest to his abs.

"Layla," he says, his voice cracking like a teenage boy as he reaches for me.

Shaking my head, I demand, "No. Keep your hands on the table so I can do my job."

His eyes flare, pooling with liquid gold and driving me forward. Lowering my hands I glide them over his thighs, my thumbs sliding inward and barely grazing his dick. "Fuck, Layla," he groans.

My confidence growing, my hand cups his balls and rubs his hard shaft over his underwear, unintelligible expletives coming through his teeth. Grabbing his underwear, he lifts his hips and I slide them down, dropping them to the floor. Standing back for a moment as his long, thick cock bounces free.

My tongue peeks out hungry, Levi's chest heaving as he watches my every move. Nudging his legs apart, I step between them. Wrapping my hand around his dick, I grip it firmly, and drag it from root to tip, precum dripping out as his head falls back, a groan falling from his lips.

"I want to touch you," he begs.

"No. You'll have to wait for that," I insist, gliding my hand back up his shaft, I cup his balls and drop to my knees. Licking the tip, I taste his salty cum and suck him completely into my mouth until he hits the back of my throat.

"Holy shit, Layla," he rasps.

His desire spurs me on. Relaxing my jaw, I suck him deep, drawing him in and out of my mouth. My hands join in, one holding the base of his cock and the other playing with his balls, feeling them quickly expand.

My nipples strain towards him and heat pools low in my belly, my own desire for him building. I moan over his dick, the vibrations adding to the sensation as I continue to work him, licking, sucking, touching.

He grips my ponytail, holding my head, his fingers trembling on my scalp. "Fuck, Layla, I'm going to come, baby."

My hands move to his firm ass and I hold him to me, doing everything I can to make him lose control. Then he does, exploding, a hot stream of salty cum shooting into my mouth. Licking, and swallowing, I keep my mouth sealed over him, sucking him dry. Then, I lick my lips clean and fall back on my heels with a small smile as he stares at me through hooded eyes. "Was that okay? Anything like your fantasy?"

He bursts out laughing, his arm falling over his face. "You are fucking perfect, Layla Romano. Absolutely, perfect."

Epilogue

Levi

Staring down at my hand, I admire my ring, still in shock that we beat the Lions in the World Series last season. Being one of the closing pitchers during the series against my former team brought a mix of emotions. Some of the men have remained good friends, while others I could do without. Besides, they were the ones who traded me, but with this on my hand, I no longer harbor hard feelings.

The ring is yellow and white gold adorned with our Mustang Logo created with diamonds, rubies and sapphires in the center and the words, World Champions circling it. The year is emblazoned on one side with previous wins listed below and our stadium on the other with National written in script over the stadium. Inside is personalized with my name, number, and position.

Now that we're headed into the next season, it's time to look forward. It's time to put a ring on Layla's finger and I'm nervous as hell. We've talked about the future, but actually proposing has me trembling. If I can close out a game in the World Series, I can ask the love of my life to marry me.

Taking a deep breath, I stride into the training room, smiling at the sight of Layla standing at the counter doing paperwork. She's dressed in black leggings, a thin ivory sweater and sneakers with her hair pulled back in her familiar ponytail. As I step into the room, she lifts her gaze, her eyes sparkling and a wide smile brightening her flawless features giving me goosebumps. "Hi, Levi."

"Hi, beautiful." Blushing, she looks away. "I need to steal you for a little while. Are you almost done?"

"I'll finish up for you, Layla," Jordan, one of her colleagues offers. I spoke to Bill earlier to share my plans and he said his staff would be happy to help however they could. I'm grateful this is one of those ways.

"You don't have to do that," Layla argues as expected.

"I'm waiting for Calabra to show up anyway. It gives me something to do."

"Okay. Thanks."

She reaches for her bag and I wave her off. "We can come back for your things."

"Okay," she says dragging out the word, her eyes narrowing.

Holding out my hand, she takes it and I entwine our fingers together. Lifting her hand to my mouth, I brush my lips over it and lower it between us feeling her stare.

"Are you all right, Levi?"

"Yeah, why?"

"You seem edgy."

Forcing a laugh, I claim, "I'm fine. I promise."

She quirks her brow but doesn't push. As I take a step down the tunnel leading to the baseball field, her steps falter. "We're going on the field?"

"Yes, but don't worry, we have permission."

Stepping out onto the ballfield with the stadium lights illuminating the diamond, she looks around in awe. "I've never been out here when it's empty like this. It's beautiful."

"So are you."

Giggling, she teases, "Such a charmer."

"Only for you, Layla." She grins, letting go of my hand and spinning around in a slow circle, taking it all in. My eyes never waver from her. The way she finds beauty and joy in the small moments is one of the reasons I love her.

"Come on," I prompt, holding my hand out once again. "I want to show you my view when I'm playing."

"Okay," she readily agrees, clasping my hand.

Strolling towards the pitcher's mound, my hands start to sweat, my heart pounds and tingles crawl up my throat. We step up on the mound together and she releases my hand, smirking. "How's my form?" she asks, her tone teasing. Then, she proceeds to pretend to pitch.

"You're pitching?" I laugh. "Are we switching rolls, now?"

"Not exactly a switch. I'm not your coach."

"Technically, no, but you are in all the ways that truly matter."

"Levi," she murmurs, the soft sound like a caress, calming my nerves.

Staring into her eyes, a smile curves my lips. "You're so damn smart, Layla, I'd be crazy not to listen to you."

Giggling, she reminds me, "You didn't think that the day you met me."

"Am I ever going to live that down?"

She shrugs, giving me a mischievous grin. "I'm here, so I think I got past it...eventually."

Chuckling, I concede, "Well, you sure know how to put me in my place. I know you won't take shit from me and that's the way it should be. You challenge me in so many ways and it makes me want to be a better man."

"I think you're already a good man, Levi."

My heart clenches. This woman. "Maybe because I have a good woman by my side and I would be honored if you would stay by my side for the rest of my life."

"That's where I want to be, with you beside me," she says not understanding where I'm going with this making me laugh.

"What's so funny?" she asks, puzzled.

Stepping towards her, I cup her cheek, giving her a chaste kiss. "You. You always know how to make me laugh."

Trailing my hand from her cheek and down her arm, I grip her hand with both of mine as I drop down on one knee, realizing it may be the only way to convey how I'm feeling. "I'm not doing this right."

Her eyes widen to the size of saucers and her chest heaves. "Levi?"

"Layla, I'm so damn in love with you. I love playing baseball but you are what makes the game of life worth living. Please, do me the honor of becoming my wife. Layla Romano, will you marry me?"

She gasps. Keeping one hand clasped with hers, I reach down with the other and dig the ring out of my pocket, her ring. Holding it up, I meet her teary gaze, mine open, vulnerable and full of love and hope. "Please, marry me."

A broad smile spreads across her face, her eyes shining. "Yes, Levi. Yes, I'll marry you."

Rising, I exhale in relief, and drag her into my arms. With a grin plastered across my face, I cradle her head in my hands and seal our mouths together, kissing her hard, almost frantic. Cheering rings through the speakers, startling us both, causing us to rear back.

Looking up towards the booth, Gabe's voice echoes around us, "Congratulations, Sis!"

We both burst out laughing and she looks at me, arching her brow. "I needed help to make this happen, so Gabe is watching from the booth and filming it for your mom."

Grinning, she stares at me, her eyes bright with emotion. "I love you, Levi."

My heart clenches like it does every time I hear those words leave her mouth. "I love you, too. You're stuck with me, now," I tease making her giggle, slipping the ring on her finger.

She glances down at the yellow gold, round diamond, surrounded by smaller diamonds. "I thought we said nothing bigger than one carat?"

"It's not." I smirk and she gives me a look, calling me on my bullshit. "The center diamond is one carat. Sure, the surrounding diamonds make it about three all together, but I thought this fit us, fit *you* perfectly."

"Because it looks like a flower. Sneaky. And beautiful. And you're right, perfect," she softly admits.

"Wanna get out of here?"

"Yes, please."

The End

Acknowledgements

I need to thank my family first for always being there for me, supporting me and being my biggest cheerleaders. I'm grateful for you and love you all!

Thank you to Ariana St. Claire for having me participate in this fantastic collaboration with so many wonderful authors. I truly enjoyed working with you and being part of Love Canyon and their book club with so many different Blind Date #BOOK-BOYFRIENDS. You set the story up perfectly with the first two books in the series (#BOOKBOYFRIEND & #HOCKEYBOY, giving us the freedom to create our own. I appreciate you and thanks to Dragonfly Design for the beautiful cover design, incorporating the model images.

A special shoutout to Darley Collins for working with me, so some of your characters (Chloe and Beck's story is a #BOYNEXTDOOR) could be a part of Levi and Layla's story. I always enjoy working with you and I adore you!

An immense thank you to my editor, Dina. I'm incredibly grateful for the way you challenge and push me to be my best. Thank you for all your time, dedication, and hard work you put into my stories. I appreciate the comments, the laughter, and the encouragement. And yes, I'm repeating myself, thank you!

Huge thank you to Luke Brennan for modeling as Levi. I had a lot of fun getting to know you and I appreciate all your stories and inspiration for the book. Thank you for spending so much time hanging at both the house and at the indoor baseball training facility to help get what we need for the cover, marketing and story. I'm also grateful for the use of your last name. Lol. Yes, that is where Levi got his last name. And thanks to writer and director, Candice Cain, for introducing us.

Judith of Judith M Riley Photography, thank you for doing this project with me. I'm thrilled we finally got to work together for a project like this! Your ideas, style, and expertise from concept to the editing floor made for a fun collaboration and photo shoot with incredible results. I hope you love it like I do. Thank you, my friend.

I'm extremely grateful to Randy and the Long Island Sports Zone for helping us out when we were hit with snow right before the photo shoot. You came in and rescued us by allowing us to come into your fantastic indoor baseball training facility, utilize equipment and space, and guide us while we took pictures. We were able to get the photos we needed for the cover and marketing, while all three of us had a great time chatting with you. Thanks!

Thank you to all my Beta and ARC readers, as well as all my readers. I appreciate every single one of you immeasurably. You are why I'm able to keep sharing my books and #BOOK-BOYFRIENDS as I follow my dreams of creating stories for all of you.

Connect with the Author

Author Website

www.nikkialamersauthor.com

All Author Links

https://linktr.ee/NikkiALamersAuthor

About the Author

Multi-Award Winning Author, Nikki A Lamers grew up in Wisconsin and lived in Florida for a few years working at "the happiest place on earth" before ending up on Long Island in New York where she now lives with her husband and their two children. She has a background in Public health and incorporates various aspects of health and wellness in her stories.

Writing, reading, coffee, chocolate, and wine all she needs alongside her friends and family. Since meeting her husband, they enjoy spending time in Maine and exploring different places, meeting new people and always looking for her next story. For her other job she freelances as a script writer, advisor and supervisor on and off set for TV, film and commercials. Now, Nikki is having fun working on her next spicy, character driven romance book!

A person with blonde hair wearing a green sweater Description automatically generated

www.ingramcontent.com/pod-product-compliance
Lightning Source LLC
Chambersburg PA
CBHW050440200726

48295CB00024B/747